"I could have just

Jake lowered his weapon, did a quick take of the hall and, seeing no one else, covered the distance between himself and Mackenzie in three seconds flat.

"Get out of here now!" he whispered vehemently, trying to push her toward the door, but she held her ground.

"I'm not leaving, Deputy Riley. I have a job to do, just like you."

"We're in pursuit of a suspect. You're in danger here, and you just might end up in the line of fire again if you're not careful. Now get out of here!"

"You're wasting time. While you're standing here arguing with me, you could be chasing him down."

Jake's eyes flashed. "You're making my job very difficult, Mackenzie."

Mackenzie frowned. "You're not making mine very easy, either."

Jake shook his head and motioned with his gun again. "We'll talk about this later. For now, stay here. Do not go any farther into this building. Do you understand? The man we're chasing is armed and isn't afraid to shoot at anything that moves."

Kathleen Tailer is a senior attorney II who works for the Supreme Court of Florida in the office of the state courts administrator. She graduated from Florida State University College of Law after earning her BA from the University of New Mexico. She and her husband have eight children, five of whom they adopted from the state of Florida. She enjoys photography and playing drums on the worship team at Calvary Chapel, Thomasville, Georgia.

Books by Kathleen Tailer

Love Inspired Suspense

Under the Marshal's Protection
The Reluctant Witness
Perilous Refuge
Quest for Justice
Undercover Jeopardy
Perilous Pursuit

PERILOUS PURSUIT

KATHLEEN TAILER

HARLEQUIN LOVE INSPIRED® SUSPENSE

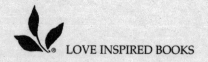

LOVE INSPIRED BOOKS

Recycling programs
for this product may
not exist in your area.

ISBN-13: 978-1-335-23218-2

Perilous Pursuit

Copyright © 2019 by Kathleen Tailer

www.Harlequin.com

Printed in U.S.A.

When thou passest through the waters, I will be with thee; and through the rivers, they shall not overflow thee: when thou walkest through the fire, thou shalt not be burned; neither shall the flame kindle upon thee.
−*Isaiah* 43:2

For my wonderful family, Jim, James, Bethany, Keandra, Jessica, Nathan, Joshua, Anna, Megan and our newest members, Daniel and Joshua. God is good, all the time! I have been blessed beyond measure.

ONE

"Really?" Mackenzie Weaver groaned and shuffled the groceries in her hands, trying to get the right key in the lock so she could get into her apartment. She'd been out all day and was bone-tired after spending hours meeting with the executives involved in her latest project for the local US Marshals office. They'd finally hammered out a deal and had approved her action plan, but it had been a long and arduous process. She shifted again, still not able to get the right key in her hand. Her purse slipped from her shoulder to her elbow, and the weight made her movements even more awkward. She juggled a bit more, and two oranges fell from her grocery bag. She let out an exasperated sigh. If she wasn't careful, the deli container of salsa she had purchased would open up and make a truly nasty mess.

Dear God, please help me make it through this day.

Her prayer was short but heartfelt. Just as she bent down to pick up the oranges, the first bullet ripped into the door frame. The sound was deafening. Splinters and paint chips spit at her as a second bullet hit just below the first. For Mackenzie, the noise from the gun was just as shocking as the sight of the bullets tearing into the wood.

She dropped her bags and hit the floor, her heart beating so hard it felt like it was about to come out of her chest. Her breath came in gasps. She scooted against the wall and then fumbled for her phone so she could call 911. She never had an opportunity. Suddenly, two rough hands pulled her to her feet and dragged her into her apartment. Another man closed the apartment door behind them.

"You idiot!" The man at the door spoke gruffly as he approached. "Why did you shoot at her? We don't want her dead! Not yet anyway, and now the noise is going to bring us company we don't need." His words sent a chill down her spine, and she started shaking.

Mackenzie tried to scream, but her captor quickly put his hand over her mouth and squeezed. His other arm was around her waist, and he pulled her roughly against him. She was sure his tight grip would leave a bruise, and his pungent body odor made the situation even worse. "Shut up, sweetheart, or you'll never speak again."

She stopped screaming but didn't stop struggling until he used the hand still clasped over her mouth to pull her head at such an awkward angle that it hurt to even move. The man was much larger than her, and even though she couldn't see his face, she could feel his polluted breath prickling the skin on her neck. When he spoke, his voice was gravelly and cruel. "Now you're learning." He pulled her head again, and she whimpered in pain. "Don't try anything stupid. Got it?"

The second man took a step forward so he was clearly in Mackenzie's line of sight. He was a large, burly man with a shock of dark hair and thick, beefy forearms. His hands were the biggest ones she'd ever seen. Even his eyebrows were bushy and accented the fierce expression on his face. He was truly formidable. "Your name is Weaver, right?" His voice was deep and menacing.

Her captor removed his hand from her face, but she didn't answer until he jerked her head once again by yanking her hair.

She whimpered in pain. "Yes."

"You make movies, right?"

"Yes."

"Where do you keep the copies?"

"Copies of what?"

The hairy man shook his head as if he was reasoning with a small child and took a step closer. "Are you *trying* to make me mad?" He pulled a pistol from his belt and put it under her chin. She could feel the cold metal biting against her skin. "I don't play games. Got it? Answer my question."

"I'm not trying to be difficult," she said softly, hoping to calm him down so she could figure out what he wanted. She was so scared it was hard to think, but she kept talking anyway. "I just don't understand what you want. I've made lots of movies, and I have all sorts of copies and edited versions of various scenes. If you tell me more about what you're looking for, I might be able to help." She glanced at her desk, which was behind the man, and he followed her eyes. He instantly turned and started searching through the drawers and filing cabinet. Papers were soon strewn about, and books and other items were thrown into disarray throughout her home office space. What were they looking for? Which of her projects had garnered their attention? None of this made any sense to her, but her confusion did little to ameliorate her fear.

Suddenly, there was a noise at the front door. "Deputy US marshal. Drop your weapons and come out with your hands up!"

The hairy man quickly looked behind her to the thug who held her captive, and then they both started backing away from the living room, pulling Mackenzie with them and using her body as a shield. They headed toward the balcony, the only other exit from her apartment.

She glanced toward the door and hope surged within her as she noticed a man with a gun quickly look around the doorjamb. He instantly took cover behind the door again, but he had to be law enforcement, just as he'd announced. She'd only gotten a quick look at him, but he had the law enforcement look—short dark hair and strong military features. There was also something vaguely familiar about him, but her mind still seemed frozen and she couldn't place him. Maybe she wasn't going to die today after all. Still, there was only one of him, and two men were holding her captive, both with loaded weapons. Anxiety formed a hard knot in her stomach, and she stumbled as the man holding her continued to pull her backward.

She was being held at such an awkward angle that she couldn't catch herself. Her abductor lost his grip, and she ended up on the floor. She expected the man to reach down and pull her up again, but instead, he left her sprawled on the tile and then turned and followed his companion out through the sliding glass door that led to the balcony. She still didn't get a look at the face of the man who'd held her but did notice dark brown hair, blue jeans and a red plaid shirt. She also saw that the hairy man had grabbed her laptop on the way out. A protest formed on her lips, but she stayed silent as she watched the two disappear by jumping off her second-floor balcony. She could buy another laptop. At this point, she was just relieved to still be alive.

Jake Riley heard the sliding door open and took another quick look. He was off duty and didn't have any backup, so he was less concerned with capturing the men with the guns than with keeping their victim safe. Seeing no one but the woman, he entered the apartment, his gun drawn.

"Stay down," he said softly as he approached, motioning with his hand. "Is there anybody else in the apartment?"

"No," she answered, "I don't think so, anyway. There were two guys that grabbed me when I came into my apartment, but they just escaped out the balcony."

Jake carefully approached the sliding door with his gun still drawn and ready. He cautiously stepped outside and quickly spotted the two suspects running through the parking lot on foot. A moment later, a black Buick four-door sedan sped away, but not before Jake was able to catch two of the numbers off the license plate. He holstered his weapon and blew out a breath. He had already called in the incident when he'd heard the gunshots, so his next move was to go to the side of the woman, who was still cowering on the floor. She had pulled herself up to a sitting position and was now leaning against her couch, hugging her legs. Jake noticed her hands were shaking as she pushed some of her long brown hair behind her ear.

"Are you hurt?"

It took a moment for her to look at him, and he imagined she was trying to compose herself. He didn't blame her. It probably wasn't every day that someone broke into her home and threatened her at gunpoint. She had to be terrified.

Finally, she glanced up at him, and his heartbeat fluttered. She had pale blue eyes, and her long brown hair framed her heart-shaped face perfectly. Her lips were a vibrant pink, and with her smooth and fresh skin she looked like a porcelain doll. He sucked in a breath. She was one of the prettiest women he had ever seen, but there was something about her... He made a conscious effort not to stare at her and was relieved that she didn't seem to notice his bad manners.

"No, I'm not hurt. Not permanently, at least." She winced as she tilted her head. "I'm a bit sore, but you arrived just in time." She looked him directly in the eye, and suddenly, recognition spread across her features. "Jake Riley?"

He raised his eyebrows, his brain frantically

searching for the woman's identity. He could only remember one person with eyes that particular color of blue, but the woman before him looked very different from what he remembered. He hazarded a guess.

"Mackenzie? Mackenzie Weaver? Is it you?"

She smiled. Yet the smile didn't quite reach her eyes, and she was quick to look away.

"Yes, it's been a few years."

Jake was floored. Mackenzie was the little sister of his best friend, Jonathan Weaver, who had been killed by a land mine in Afghanistan over four years ago. He and Jonathan had been boon companions all through high school and college, but then Jonathan had joined the army and died shortly thereafter. Mackenzie was four years younger than Jonathan and had followed the boys around like a puppy during most of their friendship. She had always wanted to be included in their escapades, but Jake and Jonathan had spent a great deal of time trying to break away from her constant pursuit. Jake had even thought that Mackenzie had a crush on him for a time when she was in high school and he was in college, but he had never been interested. Of course, the girl he remembered was nothing like the lovely woman before him. She had truly blossomed.

"The last time I saw you..."

"Was at the funeral," she finished for him.

"You've changed a bit since then," he said carefully, noting that she seemed less and less pleased that they had reunited.

"You could say that," she said, still not looking directly at him. "I've lost my braces and gained a few pounds. And I finally let my hair grow out. I guess you could say I'm all grown-up."

The girl Jake remembered had been a skinny tomboy with short hair, braces and a wardrobe filled with jeans, sports T-shirts and jerseys. The lady before him looked nothing like he remembered, with the exception of those penetrating, lovely blue eyes. She now had wonderful curves and was dressed in a pretty floral shirt that accented her femininity. "That's an understatement. You look amazing."

She shifted, apparently uncomfortable with his compliment. "I'm sure they would have killed me if you hadn't come along. Thank you for arriving when you did."

He nodded at her and turned away, still hoping that she didn't notice how much she had affected him. He met people nearly every day in his job as a deputy marshal, both old and new acquaintances, strangers and friends, but it had been quite a while since someone had garnered his attention so acutely for something other than breaking the law.

Her eyes. That was what got him. They were such an unusual shade of blue. They reminded him of the morning sky right after the sun came up. He kicked himself mentally. Morning sky? Yep. He was definitely slipping. What had gotten into him? Not one to lose focus normally, Jake quickly forced his thoughts back to the welfare of the victim and stopped thinking about the past and how much Mackenzie had changed. Besides, it was obvious that she wanted to keep the past in the past. Their shared history had ended when her brother died. Jake took a breath.

"Sure thing. I was visiting a friend who lives a couple of apartments down when I heard the gunshots. I think I scared the intruders away before they did too much damage." He gave her a reassuring smile. "Why don't you catch your breath while I call in to the office and give them the update." He busied himself with his phone and then gave dispatch the news about the men's escape and the vehicle, knowing the report would be shared with the local authorities. When he turned back, he noticed that Mackenzie had pulled herself up and was heading toward the door on shaky legs.

He quickly stored his phone. "Whoa. Where are you headed?"

She turned. "I just thought I'd grab my purse and groceries from the doorstep before I have any other visitors."

He nodded and motioned toward the couch. "Why don't you take a seat and let me get those for you?"

She shrugged. "I can get them. This may sound kind of weird, but I need to do something to work off this adrenaline." She took a step, but her legs seemed to give out underneath her. Jake reached her just in time to keep her from crashing to the floor. He swung her up into his arms and breathed her in. Was that lilacs? Or maybe jasmine? He wasn't an expert on perfumes, but he did know one thing: she smelled as good as she looked. The tomboy he remembered had totally disappeared.

She leaned against him, and he tried to ignore how comfortable she felt in his arms. It was a strange sensation for him, and once again he quickly tamped

down the attraction he was experiencing. He was off
duty, sure, but this woman was a victim of a crime,
and despite the fact that they had known each other
growing up, he was here as a law enforcement officer. He also wondered what her brother, Jonathan,
would think if he knew how Jake was reacting to his
little sister. Would he have been indifferent, or would
he have warned Jake to stay away? He mentally gave
himself a shake. Even if Jonathan had given him his
blessing, Jake had no interest in having a relationship
with anyone. He was shocked at his own reaction to
her. He steeled himself and carried her to the couch.
Then he gently set her down and took a step back.
"Just try to breathe easy and relax. The local police
will be here soon."

"I don't know what happened," she said softly. "All
of a sudden, my legs just wouldn't work."

"No worries," Jake reassured her. "That's a common sign of stress. You were just held at gunpoint by
two thugs. I'd say you're doing amazingly well." He
took a seat across from her. "Why don't you tell me
what happened?"

She scooted back a bit on the cushion and then
looked him in the eye again. She had always had a
toughness to her, and he was pleased to see she hadn't
been reduced to tears or hysterics. Dealing with emo-
tional victims was part of his job, but he was glad that
Mackenzie was strong and able to talk to him coher-
ently, despite what she'd just been through.

"I was trying to find the key to my door, but my
hands were full. I ended up dropping some of my
groceries, and when I bent down to pick them up, the

bullets hit the door frame above me. Then the man in the blue jeans grabbed me and pulled me into the apartment."

"Did you recognize either of them?"

"No. I've seen them before."

"Okay. Then what happened?"

"The guy in jeans held me, and the hairy one put a gun under my chin and said he wanted to know where I kept my movies."

"Your movies?"

"Yes. I'm a videographer. I make documentaries, commercials, training videos—that kind of thing."

That surprised him, but he couldn't really remember much about Mackenzie's plans when she had been in high school, and they had barely talked at Jonathan's funeral. "Did he say which of your movies he was interested in?"

"No. We didn't get that far. He started going through my desk, but I don't know if he took anything except my laptop. He grabbed that on the way out."

Jake put his hands on his hips. "Did you have anything important on that laptop?"

"I do some work on it, but most of the footage and movies are stored on portable hard drives. That seems to be what they were looking for. I guess they figured I had the files on my laptop." She paused, and Jake could see that her hands were still trembling. "I can't figure this out. I don't understand what they wanted. Nothing I've worked on has ever been controversial."

Jake heard the distant sound of sirens and knew local law enforcement would be there soon. This case probably wouldn't fall under the local US Marshals unit's jurisdiction, but it intrigued him none-theless, especially since he knew the victim. One of the criminals also looked like an escaped fugitive he had been hunting recently, and he hoped he could get Mackenzie to come down to the office to check out some mug shots, just in case the perpetrator was his man after all.

He ran his hands through his hair and sighed. He was relieved he'd gotten there just in time and real-ized he had probably saved her life. The two crimi-nals had meant business, but since he had interrupted them, he doubted they had gotten what they were looking for. Once thing was certain in his mind—sooner or later, they would be back.

"Look, I don't think it's safe for you to stay here tonight. Once the local law enforcement team inter-views you, you'll need to find a new place for a few days, at least until we have more information. Do you have friends you can stay with until this is over?"

Mackenzie shrugged. "I guess so, but if these men didn't get what they wanted, won't they just come after me again and put my friends in danger, too, when they return? I don't want anybody else's life disrupted because of me."

She had a point. Normally he would leave it to the local police to sort this out, but he couldn't just drive away. Just then two local detectives arrived and started interviewing both Jake and Mackenzie. The entire time they were asking questions, Jake tried to tell himself it was the connection to his fugitive that had garnered his interest in this case, and by the end of the interviews, he almost believed it himself.

Almost. After Jake and Mackenzie answered all the questions, Jake pulled aside the detective in charge.

"Look, she's afraid to go stay with friends and she can't stay here. How about I take her to a local hotel and then bring her in to the local US Marshals office tomorrow so she can sit with our sketch artist? I'll share any leads she gives."

The man raised an eyebrow. "You trying to take this case away from us, Riley?"

Jake held up his hands and smiled, his slow Southern drawl salting his words. "No way. You can have the case and the paperwork. One of the perps seems an awful lot like one of my fugitives. That's all. I just think there might be some connections here, and if we share intel, we can help each other." He pulled a business card out from his wallet and handed it to the officer. "Cooperation between agencies is one of our mandates. I won't leave you out in the dark."

The detective seemed to be weighing his words, but in the end he agreed. Jake had always done his best to keep a positive, friendly relationship with the other law enforcement agencies in Tallahassee, and tonight his efforts were paying off. Although he didn't know this officer personally, he and his team had an excellent reputation with the local agencies. The way he figured it, law enforcement personnel were all on the same team—even though they served different functions. He went to Mackenzie's side. "Go ahead and pack a bag. I'll take you somewhere safe until we can figure out what's going on here."

She raised an eyebrow but then did as she was told, returning to the living room a few minutes later with a small rolling suitcase. She also grabbed a portfolio from her desk and added several papers and a couple of files from the filing cabinet. The fear was still radiating in her eyes, but he could see that she was determined to push forward and put this incident behind her as best she could. His admiration for her went up a notch. She really was tough. He liked that. It had been a long time since anyone outside of law enforcement had impressed him on any level. He was used to dealing with the dregs of society, and Mackenzie's strength was a welcome ripple in a sea of viciousness he dealt with on a constant basis.

He started leading her out to his car. "So here's the plan. I'll take you to a hotel for the evening, one that our office uses a lot. We know we can trust the folks that run it. Then tomorrow morning, I'll pick you up around eight a.m. and bring you to my workplace so you can describe those two men to our sketch artist and maybe look at some mug books. Will that work for you?"

She nodded. "That will do nicely. I actually already have a meeting scheduled there tomorrow anyway. I can do both in one fell swoop."

Jake raised his eyebrows, surprised. "Really? Anything you care to share?"

"My new video project is about the working of the local US Marshals office. I've been hired to do a documentary for them. I was already scheduled to meet with Chief Deputy US Marshal J.T. Austin. He runs the unit I've been assigned to work with. Do you know him?"

Her words stopped Jake cold. He froze and turned

slowly to meet her eyes. "J.T. Austin is my boss." He tilted his head and narrowed his eyes. "You're doing a movie about our office?" He could tell the gruffness of his voice shocked her, but he couldn't seem to help himself. Surely she was mistaken. His boss wouldn't really sanction this type of project, would he? A documentary would put his life and the lives of others who worked with him at risk. They didn't need the exposure, and they didn't certainly need to be worrying about the safety of someone who was following them around while they were doing a very dangerous job. Jake also had a full caseload and a heap of work on his desk. He didn't have the time to push all of that aside to help with something as extraneous as a public service video.

"Yes, it's all been arranged. They didn't tell you I was coming?"

"No, they neglected to mention that." Again, his voice was frosty, even to his own ears. "I'm sure we can sort it out tomorrow, though. There's *no way* you're making a documentary of my unit. That's just not gonna happen." He'd make sure of that. He'd set Mackenzie Weaver up with the mug shot books and then meet with J.T. and voice his concerns. Jake Riley wasn't going to have any documentary made about him or the work he did, even though the videographer was an old family friend who had become a beautiful woman. He'd put a stop to the film the first thing in the morning.

TWO

Mackenzie dared another glance behind her and opened the door to the local office of the US Marshals. As she entered the building, she wasn't sure if she was being watched or not. But she couldn't shake the feeling that someone had their eyes on her and was paying attention to her every move, despite the presence of Jake Riley, who followed just a few steps behind. Last night she had stayed at the hotel suggested by Jake, but she had been truly surprised at the change in his attitude, which seemed to have gotten distinctly frostier once she'd mentioned the documentary. He'd turned into an iceberg in two minutes flat, and arriving to pick her up this morning, he hadn't said more than a handful of words to her or even met her eye.

She shouldn't really have been surprised at his behavior. As a kid, she had done her best to garner Jake's interest, but he had largely ignored her. Nothing had changed. Sure, they were both adults now, but it was painfully obvious that he still found her to be a nuisance. His distaste for her seemed even worse than when she had been following him around as a teenager. She didn't know what she had done to offend him so, but at this point, she didn't want to dwell on it. She had moved on years ago.

Maybe she was just being too sensitive. She hadn't slept very well last night. The feel of the man's gun under her chin was still too real, and the entire experience from yesterday still had her nerves on edge. But life had to go on, and she had two meetings in this office today—one with Jake Riley to look at mug shots, if he still wanted her to do so, and one with the chief to go over her action plan and start the wheels turning on her video project. As she expected, Jake Riley disappeared soon after their arrival at the building, so she asked for the chief at the front desk and was soon ushered back into a small conference room.

J.T. Austin, Chief Deputy US Marshal, came in with a warm smile and his hand out, ready to shake. He was a large man who exuded authority, with a tough-as-nails appearance. Yet his smile was genuine, and Mackenzie felt instantly at ease, incredibly glad that he was more receptive to her project than Jake Riley was. She stood to greet him and then sat back down and pulled out her portfolio.

"I'm so glad we're going to be working together, Chief Austin. I've heard great things about your unit and its amazing closure rate. You must have a truly excellent team."

"We do indeed," Austin agreed.

The door opened and Jake Riley reappeared. Mackenzie smiled at him but was met with a scowl. He still refused to meet her eye.

"I believe you already know Deputy Marshal Riley," Austin intoned.

Mackenzie was a bit flustered by Jake's icy expression, but she took it in stride. "Yes, he actually saved my life last night. A couple of men broke into my apartment and held me at gunpoint, but Deputy Marshal Riley scared them off before they could do any serious damage."

Austin raised an eyebrow. "I'm sorry to hear that."

He leaned back as Jake took a seat at the conference table. "Looks like you were in the right place at the right time, Jake." He smiled. "Mackenzie Weaver is the videographer we are working with to create our documentary. We'd been keeping the project under wraps until we worked out all the details, but now that we have a contract in place, we're ready to move forward. Ms. Weaver is making a one-hour special that will be broadcast on one of the biggest networks in the country. It should bring the agency some wonderful exposure from a media standpoint and may even help us with our budget requests. The more the legislature knows about what we do and how we do it, the better likelihood we have of getting properly funded. This movie is really important to us and will make a big impact. It's good to have her." He turned to Mackenzie. "Ms. Weaver, I've assigned you to Jake and his team so you can make your documentary. He'll be showing you the ropes and answering your questions as you go through the filming process."

Mackenzie expelled a breath, hoping her disappointment didn't show. She'd hoped Chief Austin had been planning to assist her personally, especially after

Jake's negative comments the night before. She dared another glance at Jake and was still surprised at his frigid expression. He obviously didn't want to be working with her. The question was, why? Had she said or done something last night to turn him off or insult him? Did he still think of her as a lovesick tomboy from high school? She needed his cooperation for this film to become a success. She decided to put her best foot forward and let her professionalism shine. "I'm so pleased to be working with you, Deputy."

Austin stood. "I'll leave you two to get to work. Ms. Weaver, if you need anything, my office is just down the hall. Jake, I'll trust you to take care of Ms. Weaver and help her get her work accomplished. I'm already anxious to get some popcorn and watch the final version!" He shook Mackenzie's hand again, clapped Jake on the back and left the room.

Once they were alone, Jake sighed audibly. Mackenzie raised an eyebrow. "So I take it this wasn't your first choice of assignments."

"Not even close," Jake agreed in his southern drawl.

"Did you even know this project was in the works?"

"Nope. The chief must have known how I'd react. That's why he played this one close to the vest. I didn't even have an opportunity to talk to him about it this morning like I'd planned." He leaned forward. "Look, you're gonna get in our way. It's that simple. You're making my job a hundred times harder. I know the chief seems to have high hopes for this film of yours, but I sure wish you had chosen a different agency for your exposé."

"Exposé?" Mackenzie said, hoping her frustration wasn't showing. "That's hardly what I'm doing. My film will be a positive documentary about the good work that you're doing. It's designed to make the US Marshals look good—not hurt you." She shifted. "You should also know that this was your agency's idea, not mine. They sent out a request for bids, and my proposal won the contract. If I wasn't the one behind the camera, it would have just been someone else doing the work instead of me."

He seemed to ponder her words, but in the end he didn't change his expression. "Regardless, you're still going to be in my way."

"The more you cooperate, the sooner I'll be out of your hair. That's a promise," Mackenzie said, hoping her frustration wasn't coming across in her tone. There was no reason to antagonize the man, especially since he had come to her rescue just last night. Arguing with him was also a waste of time. She would just have to prove to him that her work would reflect well on his unit and the job he did. She pulled out her storyboard sheets and laid out her plans for the movie, going over the various scenes she hoped to film and giving him the narrator's script, which would tie it all together.

"This is just my initial plan. I'd like for you to read over all of this and let me know your opinion. I want to create a realistic piece—not a work of fiction. Your input is vital."

Jake gathered all the papers together in a stack but barely glanced at them. "Fine. I'll take a look as soon as I get time, if I get time." He grimaced, wanting to stay focused on doing his job and doing it well, not on making a video that he had no interest in. "For now, I would like for you to take a look at some mug shots. I think I recognized one of the guys from your attack last night, and if I'm right, he's a mean, nasty character that I really want to get off the streets. Do you mind taking a look?"

He could tell that he'd offended her by not studying the papers she'd brought, but his focus was on catching criminals, not helping make a movie for publicity. When she nodded, he quickly led her out to the bull pen where the deputies had their desks. He seated her at a long table with three large books of pictures. He left her for about half an hour and then came back once he noticed she'd flipped through the last of them.

"Did you see anyone you recognized?"

Mackenzie shook her head. "Nope, sorry. I only saw one of them for a few seconds as he was leaving, and the other one didn't look like any of the guys in these books."

Jake was frustrated by the news but handed her a stack of flyers. Each page showed a fugitive's picture and had a short description. "Try these. Maybe you'll see him in there."

She took the flyers and started thumbing through them. Suddenly, she became animated and held up a picture. "That's him! That's the hairy one that put the gun under my chin. I'll never forget those eyes for the rest of my life."

Jake took the paper, his suspicions confirmed. The photo was of Carter Beckett, a thief and murderer who had robbed a bank in Cairo, Georgia, and killed a convenience store clerk in Tallahassee. He had been on their local most-wanted list for almost two years. "Good work, Ms. Weaver." He was so pleased he'd gotten a lead on Beckett that his negative attitude melted a bit. "Look, I'm glad you're okay after everything you went through. I'll call the local police that worked the scene last night and give them the update. Once we catch him, we'll need you to come down again and pick him out of a lineup for us."

"No problem. I'm glad I could help." She smiled. "And don't forget, I'll be here anyway, working on the movie."

He gave a small, humorless laugh. "Yeah, I guess you will." His feelings warred within him. He still wasn't happy about the movie, but by identifying Beckett, Mackenzie had given him the first big lead in the case, and he did need her help. He *had* to work with her if he was going to make any progress, whether he liked it or not. His cell phone rang, and he excused himself and answered.

"Riley."

"Marshal, this is Kevin Bourdain with the Tallahassee Police. We met yesterday?"

"Sure, I remember. I was about to call you. Ms. Weaver just identified one of the perps who attacked her yesterday. He's a local boy named Carter Beckett. I'll send over his sheet in a minute or two."

"Sounds good. I'll take a look. In the meantime, I'm calling because we've had another incident at the Weaver apartment. Someone broke in and ransacked the place. They tried to torch the apartment, too, but thankfully, the entire building didn't go up in flames. There isn't much left in her living room. We're here now and are looking for Ms. Weaver. It sounds like she's okay and with you, but we just wanted to verify her safety."

Jake glanced at Mackenzie. "Yes, she's fine. We're just finishing up with the mug shots. Do you want me to bring her over?"

"That would be great. We need her to take a look around and let us know what's missing. Maybe she can give us some insight into these crimes, as well."

"Sure thing. We'll be right there." He hung up and gestured at Mackenzie. "I'm sorry to say there was another break-in at your apartment and a fire." He put his hand on her shoulder, trying to offer her some comfort. "I'm really glad you didn't stay there last night."

Mackenzie's face showed alarm, and she stood rapidly and started stowing her paperwork. "Was anybody hurt?"

"Thankfully, no. The perpetrators ransacked your apartment, though. I'm also guessing the guys that started the fire were only amateur arsonists, because the flames didn't spread beyond your apartment. The fire department has everything under control, and police have secured the scene. They want me to take you over right now to let them know if anything was stolen."

"Are you sure it's safe?"

"Yes, they wouldn't ask me to bring you if it wasn't."

The answer didn't seem to persuade her, and he could see her hands had started to shake like they had yesterday at the crime scene. He softened his tone. "The perpetrators are probably long gone, especially with all those police and fire department personnel walking around. And I'll be with you the whole time. I promise."

This answer seemed to help, and he noticed a grateful look in her eyes. "Was it the same guys that attacked me?"

"I don't think they know yet, but we'll find out for sure once we get there if they have any leads."

He noticed her skin turn a shade paler, but to her credit, she gathered the last of her things and headed toward the door. "Okay. Let's do this."

As they rode over to her place almost in total silence, he couldn't help observing that a wonderful smell wafted over from Mackenzie. It was again some sort of flowery perfume that Jake couldn't identify, but it tantalized his senses and was sweet without being overwhelming. He tamped down his reaction and tried to focus on his driving.

When they pulled up into the parking lot of her complex, Jake kept a vigilant eye on their surroundings. He wasn't looking for anything in particular, but his years with the US Marshals had trained him to be a keen observer and to always expect the unexpected. He noticed a blue SUV parked about halfway down the block that seemed to have a driver sitting in the car, and he kept an eye on the vehicle to see if the man would stay inside or drive away. The driver could be harmless, or he could be involved. All of the other parked cars appeared to be empty. He noted the first three numbers of the SUV's license tag, which was all he could see, just in case.

He did a fast parking job but turned to Mackenzie

before getting out of the car. "Does anything look out of place to you here? It may be hard to tell, but it's possible that whoever did this might still be hanging around. I want you to be careful and aware of your surroundings at all times."

"I thought you said it was supposed to be safe to come back."

"You're right, I did, and with all these cops everywhere, I'm sure the perps are long gone. Still, you're the one who lives here, so you would know better than anyone else if something strange is going on. All I'm saying is that I want you to keep your eyes open. If you see something that doesn't sit right with you, then you need to share it immediately. Okay?"

She nodded just as the first bullet ripped into the seat by her shoulder. She screamed as the second bullet cracked the windshield. Jake didn't wait for the third. He gunned the engine and flew out of the parking lot, the tires screeching against the pavement in protest as the back of the car fishtailed to the left. He heard other officers yelling and returning fire, but his primary concern was keeping Mackenzie safe. "Get down!" he yelled, pushing her lower on the seat. He stomped on the gas, feeling the surge of the engine as it roared and jolted him out of the parking lot and into the traffic on the main road. Another bullet shattered the rear window of the car just as he maneuvered around a large truck that would shield them temporarily from the onslaught. Somebody definitely wanted Mackenzie Weaver dead. But why?

THREE

Jake spun the steering wheel as the velocity from the swerve slammed his body against the car door. The tires screeched in protest, but he kept the car on the road. They darted ahead of two other cars and then swung back into their own lane. He checked the rearview mirror. The blue SUV was now a few cars behind them. It was slowly gaining on them but had gotten stuck behind an antique VW bug and a minivan. Jake couldn't see who was driving, but he did note that there were two of them in the vehicle instead of just the one he had originally seen. He glanced over at Mackenzie, who was still scrunched against the seats, and he touched her shoulder lightly. "Hold on. I'm going to try to put some distance between us and the guys with the guns." He punched the accelerator and felt the engine surge as the car ate up the pavement.

Mackenzie glanced up at him, and even though there was fear mirrored there, Jake also saw a level of trust. It bolstered him and made a warmth spread through him that he hadn't felt in a long time. He tamped the feelings down. He might decide to analyze them later, but right now, all he wanted to think about was getting away from that SUV. He called in on his radio and let his team know what was happening, but nobody was in the immediate area. He did hear sirens in the distance, however, so he was sure the local police who had been working the apartment building were giving chase. They had to have heard the gunshots and his reports on the radio.

Jake took another look in his rearview mirror. The blue SUV had finally passed the two slower vehicles and was moving closer. Jake swerved to pass a red sedan and barely missed a truck coming toward them in the other lane. Tires squealed, and the truck's driver laid on his horn as Jake maneuvered back into their own lane just in the nick of time to avoid a head-on collision. He looked back again in his mirror and saw a hand holding a pistol come out of the passenger side of the SUV. The perp fired two more shots at them, and Jake swerved to miss the flying bullets. The car skidded on some gravel in response, but he kept control of the wheel. A plume of smoke rose near the asphalt as the tires protested. Despite his maneuvering, one bullet caught the back of the vehicle near the trunk, but the other went wild. The man fired another shot that missed and then pulled his arm back inside the window. Suddenly the SUV turned onto a side road, abandoning the chase. It didn't take Jake long to figure out why—two police cars were coming up fast behind them, lights and sirens blazing.

"Need some help, Deputy, or should we follow the

perps?" asked the deep male voice that came over the police radio.

"We're good. Stay with the perps. We'll rendez-vous back at the Weaver apartment."

Mackenzie's eyes rounded. "Are you insane? You want to go back there?"

"Don't you? The guys with the guns will be in custody soon, and we still need you to take a look around and see what's missing."

Mackenzie sat up. She turned to look behind her and then brushed some of the broken glass off her shirt. She paused before answering, apparently giving the idea a great deal of thought. Finally, she nodded. "I guess so, if you think it's safe. I mean, I want to see what's left of the place, but I'm not too anxious to get shot at again. Being shot at may happen to you every day, but it's a new experience for me." She was quiet for a moment but then gave him a smile that surprised him. "It's too bad I didn't have my camera. This would have made some great footage."

Her comments made him smile in spite of himself. Spirit. That was what she had. A good dose of spirit. He admired that. She'd always had more than her fair share. Even though he found it appealing, however, her bravado wasn't enough to change his mind about her video project. His smile disappeared. He was still adamantly opposed to her filming his team in action. He pushed thoughts of her movie to the back of his mind. Right now, all he wanted to do was focus on finding Carter Beckett and his cohorts and putting them behind bars. This lead had sent that case to the top of his list.

He slowed the car and made a U-turn, and a few minutes later, they were back in her apartment, stepping gingerly over the charred remains of her end tables. According to the fire inspector at the scene, the blaze had been started in the kitchen and had spread into the living room. Unfortunately, it had damaged her desk and everything on and near it. Jake looked over at Mackenzie, wondering how she was going to cope with the loss of so many of her belongings. It was bad enough to have someone break in and ransack your apartment, but the fire had ruined some very expensive-looking equipment, as well. He felt bad for her. He didn't know how he would be handling this kind of loss if he were in her shoes.

Mackenzie's heart seemed to stop as she made her way into the damaged areas. Her flat screen TV had basically melted and was now a large lump of black plastic sitting on a charred wooden stand. The fire had gone up the walls and left black marks where her pictures had been hanging, and the tiled floor was littered with ash, soot and the residue from the fire extinguishers. A horrid smell of chemicals and burnt wiring permeated her senses and all of her belongings.

Finally she turned and viewed what she had been dreading—the damage to her video and audio equipment. She had an office set up in one corner of the living room, and besides her desk, she had two large video monitors, an editing board and a computer where she did the majority of her work. To the left had been the audio equipment stacked in an adjustable shelving unit and to the right a large wooden filing cabinet had stood. It was now all a heap of twisted metal and melted plastic, totally destroyed by the fire. It was as if someone had poured gasoline directly on her equipment to ensure that it would burn.

The loss was like a literal blow to her stomach, and she rubbed her abdomen absently as nausea spun and twisted inside her. She was thankful that the fire hadn't spread into the bedrooms or other apartments in the complex, but the ruined equipment represented her livelihood, and she felt the loss keenly. She was insured, but it would take a while to deal with the insurance company and rebuild her setup. Fortunately, her video camera and lighting equipment were all stored at her assistant's house. If those had been in the apartment today, her business would have come to a total standstill.

"I'm sorry you lost so much." Jake offered.

Mackenzie nodded, appreciating his words, especially since he wasn't a fan of her project. She took a deep breath and tried to focus on the positive. She had always been extremely self-sufficient and self-reliant. She would weather this storm, even though it seemed more like a hurricane. "Thanks. At least no one was hurt. That's the main thing. This is all stuff. I'm sorry to see it go, but it is replaceable."

She said a prayer of thanksgiving. God would see her through this catastrophe. She still had much to be grateful for. It would take time and effort, but she would rebuild, and God would be there to help her along the way and remind her about what was truly important in life if she got frustrated by the process.

Jake took a step in her direction. "I know it's hard to tell with all of the fire damage, but the local police want to know if you can tell them if anything is missing. It might help us figure out why someone has targeted you."

"Okay. I'll take a look around." She stepped over some unidentifiable object on the tile and moved toward the bedrooms. Both were untouched by the fire. She opened a few drawers and pulled open the closets in the guest bedroom, but everything looked the same as when she had left it. She moved to her own bedroom and did the same checks. "I don't know what they were after. There doesn't seem to be anything missing." Her eyes moved to the cherished picture of her and her brother, Jonathan, which was on top of her dresser, and she touched the corner of the frame. At least the photo had been spared.

"That's a great shot," Jake asked, motioning to the photo of the two siblings smiling in the sunlight.

Mackenzie turned at his words. "That was the day I got my braces removed. I was thrilled. Jonathan took me out to dinner to celebrate. It was a big day."

"I can tell. That's a big smile." He paused. "Look, you need to pack a bag—a bigger one this time, and I'd also take your valuables, just in case. You'll need to stay at the hotel until we can get a handle on this."

Mackenzie shrugged. "I guess I'll go back there for now, but I can't stay there forever." She went to her closet, pulled out a suitcase and started packing. A few minutes later, she heard Jake approach behind her.

"Do you have any idea why someone would want to destroy your equipment?" Jake asked.

Mackenzie folded a shirt and placed it in the suitcase. "No idea at all. None of this makes any sense. I've never faced any opposition to my work. The biggest problem I've had is competing bids with other production companies, and really that's just part of the business and nothing out of the ordinary."

"The things Beckett said when he threatened you and the damage to the equipment make me think it does have something to do with your work—even if the answer isn't readily apparent." He leaned against the door frame. "Tell me about your last couple of projects. What were they about?"

Mackenzie answered as she packed. "I started the year with a training video for the Southern Pines Pediatric Clinic, and then I did a couple of commercials for the children's museum downtown. After that, I finished an overview of the governor's literacy program and a series of productions for the state's tourism campaign. My latest work was an hour-long documentary on homeless children and runaways." She closed the suitcase. "Nothing I've worked on was controversial."

"Have you turned over all the final copies to the buyers?"

"Yes, all except for the homeless children project. I just have a tad more editing to do before it's finalized."

"How did the fire affect your copies? Did everything get destroyed?"

Mackenzie shook her head. "The equipment is ruined, but I have two sets of hard drives where the files are stored. One was here in the filing cabinet and that is probably completely destroyed, but I have a second set I keep in a safety deposit box at the bank. I update the files weekly in both locations. I've always done it that way—just in case of hurricanes or whatever. I've been playing with the idea of using cloud storage, but I'm still exploring that. I'm not convinced of the security."

Jake nodded and then motioned for her to wait when his cell phone rang. He turned to answer it, and her own phone rang at the same time. She recognized her parents' number and hesitated. Could she handle a call from them right now? She hadn't told them about the men breaking into her apartment yesterday, but it would be hard hiding the fire from them, especially if she wouldn't be home for a while. She glanced at Jake, who was still deep in conversation, then back at her own phone, which was still ringing. Finally, she accepted the call.

"Hello, Dad," she said on hearing her father's voice.

"Mackenzie, I've got the best news for you!"

"Oh, really? What's up?" she asked.

"Do you remember Miller from the advertising firm? I was talking to him yesterday and mentioned you were looking for a new job. He actually has an opening and would like to set up an interview! Isn't that fantastic? All you have to do is give him a call."

Mackenzie's heart plunged. Neither of her parents felt that making movies constituted a "real" job, and they were constantly sending their disapproval her way, along with various job offers that they felt would help her settle down and take life more seriously.

Mackenzie loved them both dearly, but she wasn't about to give up her production company. She enjoyed her work and found fulfillment in the process. Her parents, however, couldn't seem to understand. She was convinced that they wouldn't be happy with her career choices until she was locked into a nine-to-five schedule with benefits and a hefty retirement plan. After Jonathan's death, their pressure had increased rather than lessened. She was now their only living child, so all their hopes and dreams rested heavily on her shoulders.

"Thanks, Dad, but I'm doing fine with my current job. I'm really not looking for anything new right now."

"But it has a great starting salary. Don't you want to at least talk to him about the opportunity? It might be too good to pass up. It's entry-level, but it has some exciting possibilities." The disapproval was heavy in his voice, and Mackenzie struggled with the desire to hang up on him. His censure was difficult to hear after everything else that had happened the last couple of days, and she was already stressed from being shot at again and having her belongings burned to a crisp. Not to mention the volatile relationship she had with Jake. She could usually handle her father's criticism and take it with a smile, but today it seemed even harder than normal to keep the optimism in her voice. *God, give me strength.*

She steeled her voice. "Dad, I'm sorry, but that's really not the path I want to take right now. I've had a fire at my apartment, and most of my equipment has been damaged. I really need to work on getting my production company up and running again so I can meet my current contracts."

"A fire? Were you hurt?"

"No, Dad, I'm fine, but like I said, I lost my board and audio equipment. It just happened, and the police and firemen are here right now sorting through everything. I really need to go so I can finish up with them and assess the damage."

There was a pause as her father absorbed everything, but then he pushed again. "Mackenzie, maybe this is the perfect time to talk to Miller after all. With your equipment damaged, it might be the best time to get a real job and put this filming behind you. You had a good run and worked on a few fun projects, but this job with Miller could turn out to be a great career. It has health benefits, a great dental plan..."

Mackenzie's head started pounding, and she rubbed her face absently. "I'm sorry, Dad, but the police really need to ask me some more questions, so I'd better go. I realize I've got a lot of work to do to rebuild my business, but that's where I want to focus my time and efforts right now. If you run into Miller again, please thank him for his time, but I'm really not interested."

"All right." She could still hear the disappointment that was heavy in his voice. "Where are you staying? Are you safe?"

"Yes, Dad, I'm safe," Mackezie answered, relieved that the conversation had shifted from her employment situation. "The US Marshals office here is helping me and has gotten me set up in a nearby hotel. I'll have to find a new apartment, but I'll let you know once I'm settled."

"All right, then. Call if you need us. We'll come help you move if you'd like."

"Sure thing. I'll let you know once I've decided where I'm headed. Bye, Dad." She hung up and sighed. Her parents meant well, but they had never really understood her work and career choices. They thought making movies was a great hobby, but certainly not a full-time occupation. With every passing year, they seemed to get more concerned about her future, and nothing she told them ever seemed good enough to please them. She desperately wanted their approval but, at this point, she was unsure if she would ever actually get it. Their lack of support ate at her yet also drove her to prove them wrong and work even harder at becoming a success. She was going to make a name for herself in the film business, and one day, she would garner their support. She glanced back over at her ruined equipment. Right now, that day seemed very far away indeed.

FOUR

A hand on her shoulder brought Mackenzie out of her contemplations, and she turned to see Jake.

"Good news. The local boys caught the two men that were shooting at us." He showed her his phone, which had a mug shot of a man with dark hair and eyes. "Do you recognize this man?"

Mackenzie shook her head. The man's face didn't set off any bells, but the emptiness in his eyes scared her. He looked like someone that would hurt her with no qualms whatsoever.

Jake swiped the screen and showed her another picture. "What about him? Have you seen him before?"

This man's face was narrower, and he had a large mole near his mouth. His lips formed a menacing sneer.

"Nope, I don't know him. Sorry."

Jake nodded and stored his phone. "Okay. They're running criminal history checks on them now. The first one I showed you is a known associate of Beckett's. It's likely that this is all tied together. All we have to do now is figure out how." He reached down, grabbed her suitcase and then motioned toward the door. "Let's get you out of here." He walked her into the living room, and after updating the two policemen, took her arm and led her toward the car.

"Will I be allowed back in there at some point to get the rest of my things?" Mackenzie asked as he opened the passenger door for her.

"Sure, at some point. Both the fire department and the police have to finish their investigations first. It'll take a few days. Hopefully, by then we'll have a handle on what's going on here." He closed the door, put her suitcase in the back seat, walked around the car and got in the driver's side. "Everything about your projects sounds innocuous, except for maybe the homeless children documentary. Tell me about that." He started the engine and pulled out of the parking lot but looked over at her expectantly.

Mackenzie waited a moment before answering, wondering if they were going to be shot at a second time. Part of her wanted to stay indoors, where it might be safer, but she quickly remembered that men had broken into her apartment. There was no guarantee she was safe anywhere right now. She glanced at Jake, who also was taking a good look around them with a wary eye. At least Jake was helping her, despite the animosity he had shown her after hearing about her movie for the US Marshals.

A moment passed, then another. When nothing happened, Mackenzie took a deep breath, a wave of relief sweeping over her. She suddenly realized she had been clenching her hands. Her nails had left marks on her palms. She rubbed her hands against her jeans, trying to help the marks disappear. She thought back on her latest video project, hoping their conversation would erase some of the fear she was feeling. "Tallahassee has been experiencing a huge increase in homelessness lately, but it isn't just adults that are sleeping on the streets. Due to the recent foreclosure crisis, families are losing their homes in record numbers, and there's also a runaway component that is a big problem. A large part of the struggling population is teenagers, and I wanted to shine a light on that social issue. I'm hoping that if I ruffle enough feathers, the legislature and the Department of Children and Families will aim more of their resources into helping teens. A lot of the young adults I interviewed were foster kids who aged out of the system and didn't have a job or home to go to."

Jake turned a corner. "Who paid for that project?"

"A nonprofit charity named the Safe Harbor Group."

"I've heard of them. They're a pretty powerful advocacy group, from what I understand."

Mackenzie nodded. "Yes, they're a Florida-based organization with offices in Tallahassee, Tampa and Miami. Last year they sank a heap of money into lobbyists to get a bill passed through the Florida legislature to combat homelessness. It didn't pass, so they hired me to make a video to highlight the problem, and they are gearing up to try again next year. They want to show my documentary on the local cable channels to garner support from the public, who they hope will pressure their representatives to vote for the legislation the next time around. It's scheduled to air in about a month. I've got a small amount of editing to finish, and then I'll be sending the final versions to their home office."

"Is there any major opposition to the bill that you're aware of?"

"Only the normal issues surrounding the cost of the legislation. Everybody seems to think helping the homeless is a good idea, but nobody wants to pay the tab. In the past, this type of legislation has been full of unfunded mandates, but this time around, the bill calls for some serious money to be spent on mental health services and child welfare programs." Mackenzie suddenly sat up straighter and took a look at their location. "Instead of heading to the hotel, would you mind dropping me by my assistant's house? It's actually just around the corner from where we are now. I need to stop by and pick up my video camera and lighting equipment, and if she's home, she can probably take me back to the hotel so you won't have to. I want to take some live action shots of your team at work, starting tomorrow."

Jake frowned, and his distaste for her idea was almost palpable. She was discouraged by his attitude and thought it was time to confront him. Being shot at two days in a row had also reduced her inhibitions. She just didn't understand his hesitance. "Okay, Jake. It's obvious you don't want me to film you. What's the problem?"

Jake shrugged, and Mackenzie could tell he was trying to decide how much to say. He had been ordered by his chief to help her, but the chief couldn't make him like the idea or participate in the shots she needed for her storyboard to come to reality. She could probably make the film without his help, but it wouldn't be easy, and it wouldn't be as good. Mackenzie hoped that if he shared his concerns, maybe she could address them. The silence stretched between them, but finally he spoke.

"I have two reasons why I don't want to make this movie. Like I told you before, you'll get in our way. That puts you in danger, and it puts our officers in danger since we have to be thinking about your safety at the same time we're trying to do our job. Second, you'll make it impossible for any of us to go undercover in the future. Once our names and faces are publicized, we'll never get that back."

Mackenzie waited, hoping for more, but Jake seemed to have become a man of very few words. She wondered fleetingly if she had ever really known him at all. "I can't solve the undercover problem short of keeping your names out of the movie and pixelating your faces anytime you're on the screen. That's not my first choice because seeing the real you would have a larger impact on the viewers, but I certainly don't want to put your lives at risk. You already do a dangerous job, and I don't want to make it worse. I can also assure you that I'll do my best to stay out of the way. Once you really look at the script and storyboard, I think you'll feel better about the project. I'm open to changes if you have some ideas. I'd really like to sit down with you tomorrow and go over my plans."

Jake shook his head. "Don't count on it."

Mackenzie pursed her lips. It was too bad that she had to have such an unwilling partner in this, but she was committed to the project and would see it through, with or without Jake's help. She surveyed him closely as he drove. His short, military-style dark brown hair framed his face perfectly, and his clean-cut features and Southern gentleman manners made him seem professional yet also approachable. If anything, he had gotten more handsome over the years. How was that possible? He was perfect for her movie and would do an excellent job of representing the US Marshals, if she could just get him to cooperate.

She snuck another look at his profile. Over the years, he had honed his muscular physique, and he probably worked out on a regular basis to keep his strong, athletic body fit. She had always thought he was good-looking, and a new whisper of attraction swept over her now as she admired the man he had become. She shook her head and tried to push it away. How ridiculous. Back in school, Jake had never re-turned her sentiment, and she had made a fool of herself around him on more than one occasion. She certainly didn't want to do so again. She forced her eyes to look out the window and watch the passing scenery. A few moments later, though, she returned to her perusal, almost without realizing it. His eyes. Those had always been his best feature. Jake Riley didn't say very much, but his intense green eyes took in everything around him, and his mind was sharp, always catching the little details that others probably overlooked. A quiet observer of all he surveyed—that was an apt description of the deputy. There was a sadness in those eyes, though—as if he had seen the worst humanity had to offer and never really recovered. She wondered what he did for fun outside the workplace or if he even had any hobbies away from the job that brought joy to his life. He'd never been a "life of the party" kind of guy, but she remembered him enjoying sports and going to movies. Now his job seemed to define him. Was there more beneath the surface?

"What about your laptop?" Jake asked, suddenly breaking her train of thought. "Did you want to stop somewhere to buy a new one? We can do that now, too, if you'd like."

The question startled her, and she abandoned her musings. "I have a Costco membership and can probably find something there. I don't need anything fancy—just something with enough speed to support my video software. I would appreciate it if we could stop, but I don't want to keep you away from the office if you need to get back."

Jake was quiet for a moment. "Actually, I'd rather take you on your errands. Until we have a better handle on the folks threatening you and what they're after, I want to make sure you're safe. That's my priority."

Mackenzie's immediate reaction was surprise, which was quickly replaced with doubt. "But I know you're really busy, and like you said, I don't want to be in your way…" His opposition to her project was already a mountain she needed to climb, and she didn't want to make it worse by interrupting even more of his work.

Jake stopped at a streetlight and turned to look her in the eye. "It's a done deal, Mackenzie. And you don't need to worry. You're a victim in the Beckett case, and I've been assigned to work with you on this film project, so either way, spending time with you is appropriate." He leaned a bit closer. "I'm going to make sure you're safe, movie or no movie." The Southern twang of his accent softened the forcefulness of his statement, but friction still sizzled in the air. She was still uncomfortable with having him serve as her escort. A moment passed as their eyes locked, but then the stoplight changed and he turned his attention back to his driving.

Jake drove the rest of the way to the warehouse store in virtual silence, but he kept a vigilant watch on Mackenzie as she shopped. She picked out a new laptop and case that would meet her needs, as well as a new portable hard drive to replace the one that had been damaged in the fire, so she could store and back up her video clips as she had before.

A few minutes later, they retrieved her camera and other equipment she needed from her assistant's house. Then they made a third stop by her safety deposit box at her bank, and she downloaded copies of all her movies onto her new hard drive, leaving the original backups in the box so they would remain safely tucked away. Jake was anxious to watch her film about homeless children to see if he could find any connections to the case, so he was glad a copy of her work still existed. Even though he wasn't thrilled to be working with her, he realized that Mackenzie and her movie project were his best leads for finding and arresting Beckett. Before he could watch the video, however, he knew he had to do something about her safety. She had already been attacked twice in twenty-four hours. He couldn't risk losing her to Beckett and his goons. As soon as they returned to his workplace, Jake led her along a long hallway. He unlocked a door and motioned for her to follow him in.

"What's this about?"

"Security. Have you ever worn a bulletproof vest before?"

Mackenzie shook her head. "No. I've never needed one before."

"Until we have Beckett behind bars, you need one." He pulled a vest off a hook, checked the tag and handed it to her. "This is a medium. Let's see if it fits. It's the smallest size we have." He helped her get it on and showed her how to tighten the straps. When he breathed in, he paused. Jasmine. It had to be jasmine in her perfume. The sweet scent distracted him once again, and he gritted his teeth. Why did this woman affect him so?

He thought back to the skinny, awkward kid whom he and Jonathan had done their best to ditch when they were in college. They could have treated her better. He felt a pang of regret.

"Wow! It's so heavy!"

"Yeah, they're definitely heavier than they look." He stepped back, trying to erase the memories and put as much space between them as possible. "I think that's the right size—at least, it's the best we can do."

Mackenzie adjusted the vest and stood up straight. "What do you think? Am I ready to go?" She flashed him a smile that sent a warm sensation from his head

to his toes. He didn't think she was purposely trying to flirt with him, but he seemed unable to resist
her innocuous grin. How could she still be smiling
after being shot at and losing all her equipment? Why
wasn't she reduced to tears and hysterics the way
most people would be?

He didn't understand. After everything that had
happened to her, Mackenzie should be stressed and
bad-tempered, but she wasn't. Even on the job, Jake
had seen so much ugliness that he now came to expect it, even from the victims. Mackenzie's attitude
was like a breath of fresh air. Yet it also irritated
him for reasons he couldn't quite identify. She was
nothing like he remembered. In fact, he was starting
to believe that he had really never known her at all.

He shook his head and leaned back in his chair,
focusing again on the vest. "You're not even close to
being ready, Mackenzie, but it will have to do." He
reached over and adjusted the straps one more time.
"You do need to tighten it a bit. We don't want it to
chafe you as you move."

Mackenzie nodded and seemed to note his adjust-
ments. Then she removed the vest since it wasn't necessary to wear it while they were in the US Marshals
office. "Okay. What next?"

"Now we're going to watch your movies and see
if we can figure out why you've become target practice for Carter Beckett and his friends."

"Got any popcorn?"

Jake raised an eyebrow at her quip but didn't smile.
Her positive attitude was such a different reaction
than what he usually experienced that it was starting

to concern him. Didn't she realize that her life was in danger? That most of her business equipment had just gone up in smoke? That she had to move and find a new place to live? Why wasn't she depressed and angry? Why wasn't she taking the threat seriously?

"Look, this is grave business, Mackenzie. Carter Beckett and his friends aren't playing a game. They're criminals, and for some reason, they've focused their attention on you. Carter is a murderer. He's also got a history of committing all sorts of other crimes. He hurts people and doesn't think twice about it. You'd be wise to take both him and his threats seriously."

His words made her eyes flash, but the smile didn't waver from her lips. "Believe me, Jake. I am very aware of the gravity of the situation. I don't get shot at every day, and I've certainly never had my apartment burned by an arsonist. In fact, this entire situation is totally new to me, and it scares me to the bone. But I'm not going to crawl into a hole and let them win, either. I'm in no hurry to die, but I'm not going to just roll over and cry 'uncle.' I've got a job to do and a life to live, and neither Carter Beckett nor his friends are going to keep me from doing either one."

Jake raised an eyebrow again but decided against continuing the argument. She was driven to succeed, and apparently nothing he said was going to change her mind. Once again, he found himself admiring her spirit, despite the fact that her attitude scared him a bit. Anybody with that much determination might also act recklessly, though, and like it or not, it was now his job to protect her—at least until her movie about his US Marshals unit was completed and the threat against her was extinguished.

Mackenzie followed him to an interview room, and they plugged in her new laptop and hard drive. A few moments later her documentary on the homeless was rolling across the screen. Jake realized she had probably seen the footage hundreds of times—both throughout the filming and then again during the editing process. This time, however, he hoped she might be looking at it with fresh eyes. Maybe one of them would see a link between her movie and the horrible events of the last two days that would bring some insight into the case at hand. Right now, the pieces just weren't fitting together.

They watched the first half hour or so without comment, but suddenly, Jake's chair fell forward. "Stop right there." He motioned to the screen where there was a kid sitting on the sidewalk in the foreground. "See that man there in the back? Can you blow up that image?"

Mackenzie looked where he was pointing, and with a few clicks on her keyboard, isolated the image. There were a few people in the background, including a couple of teenagers, but she quickly focused on the man Jake had identified and expanded the picture. Jake leaned forward to get a better look. Once it became clear, it was easy to identify Carter Beckett's features.

"That's our man," Jake said, unable to keep the excitement from his voice. "There's the link we were looking for."

Mackenzie gave him another smile. "It sure is. You

have a good eye for this. I don't think I would have even recognized him."

Jake shrugged. "I've dealt with Carter in the past on more than one occasion. You only saw him for a few minutes during a high-stress encounter." He looked closer at the screen. "Where was that shot taken?"

With a few more clicks, she expanded the view further and moved it around so the buildings were more identifiable. "We filmed this over on Mission Road. Yes, here," she said, pointing. "It looks like the address is around the 4500 block. That's an office building there, but I'm not sure what organization rents the space." She turned and raised an eyebrow. "So what's the connection? Do you think Carter Beckett was doing something illegal in that building and wanted to destroy my film so no one noticed he was at that address?"

"That's a good guess. Or maybe his activity is illegal and he just happens to be meeting someone there. In either case, I think we should head over to that office building and see if we can learn anything." He looked at his watch. "Now's a good time as any. I'll assemble the team, and we'll head on over and see what we can discover. Hopefully, we'll find Mr. Beckett himself."

FIVE

Jake dove behind a desk inside the office building on Mission Road, just as a spray of bullets showered the room, biting into the furniture and sheetrock behind him. He glanced over at Dominic Sullivan, one of the other deputy marshals on his team, who had taken refuge behind a filing cabinet. Dominic gave him the "okay" sign, and Jake said a quick prayer of thanks that neither of them had been hit. Finally, the barrage ceased and they heard footsteps in the distance running away from them. Jake made eye contact with Dominic again and then motioned and nodded as he rose to follow the suspect, his weapon ready. The two deputies started down the hallway, cautiously pursuing the gunman. They saw no one but checked each door as they went, just in case the fugitive had hidden inside one of the offices. Most of the doors were locked because it was after normal business hours, but a few were open and they carefully checked each and every room before proceeding toward the exit sign at the end of the hall. It was a slow process, but they didn't want to get ambushed or miss their quarry altogether.

When they'd arrived at the building, Carter Beckett had seen them coming and had escaped down the stairs to the third floor of the building before they could stop him. They didn't know if he was alone or if there were other hidden dangers, so they proceeded cautiously. Beckett had evaded arrest twice before, but this time they were going to make the arrest—Jake was sure of it. Right now, while Dominic and he were following the fugitive, two other deputy marshals were securing the perimeter of the building. They were slowly closing in, and the suspect had no place to go.

Jake and Dominic were almost at the end of the hallway when they suddenly heard a door slam behind them. Both men swung around, their guns pointed at the source of the noise.

"Sorry," Mackenzie whispered, her expression repentant. Her bulletproof vest with the words US MARSHAL splashed across the front seemed to swallow her, and she adjusted it as she came toward them, holding the camera with its red light blaring, recording the deputies' every move.

Jake lowered his weapon, did a quick take of the hall and, seeing no one else, covered the distance between them in three seconds flat. "I could have just shot you! Do you understand that?" he whispered vehemently, motioning with his weapon. "Get out of here, now!" He tried to push her toward the door, but she held her ground.

"I'm not leaving, Deputy Riley. I have a job to do, just like you."

"We're in pursuit of a suspect. You're in danger

here, and you just might end up in the line of fire again if you're not careful. Now, get out of here!"

"You're wasting time. While you're standing here arguing with me, you could be chasing Carter down."

Jake's eyes flashed. "You're making my job very difficult, Mackenzie."

Mackenzie frowned. "You're not making mine very easy, either."

Jake shook his head and motioned with his gun again. "We'll talk about this later. For now, stay here. Do not go any further into this building. Do you understand? The man we're chasing is armed and isn't afraid to shoot at anything that moves."

"I hear you."

Jake whirled and rejoined Dominic down the hall, very aware that she hadn't agreed to stay where he wanted her. A wave of frustration swept over him, but he tamped it back down. He glanced behind him and saw her fiddling with her camera. The woman was right about one thing. He couldn't spend any more time arguing with her without risking losing his suspect altogether, even if there were three other deputies in pursuit.

He motioned to Dominic, and the deputies turned and checked the remaining offices. The last door was unlocked and led them into a large conference-size room that was filled with copy machines, all in various stages of disrepair. Several tools were also scattered about, and a couple of cardboard boxes with parts of different sizes and shapes were on a nearby table.

A noise at the other end of the room made them

turn, and both men ducked for cover, just as another barrage of bullets rained down upon them. Bits of plastic and copy machine parts flew into the air as the bullets ripped into the machines.

A moment after the bullets stopped, Jake could just make out the sight of a door swinging closed at the far end of the room. He looked behind him, verifying again that Dominic was safe and that Mackenzie hadn't followed them and caught a stray bullet. Thankfully, Dominic wasn't hurt and Mackenzie was nowhere in sight. He grabbed the transmitter attached to his sleeve and held it up to his mouth. "Chris? We're in the northwest corner of the building. The suspect just went into the stairwell again."

"Copy that," Chris Riggs answered. "Whitney and I are down in the parking garage and have it secured. We'll head in that direction. Is he by himself?"

"Affirmative," Jake answered. "He's got a semiautomatic rifle, and he isn't afraid to use it." He paused. "The video crew is on the loose, too. Be careful." He caught Dominic's eye again and motioned with his hand, then headed for the stairwell door, knowing that Dominic had his back. Jake had been working with this group of deputy marshals for the last couple of years and was convinced they were the best team in the entire southeast. They were always there for one another, and he would lay down his life for any of them just the same.

The two moved quickly but cautiously. Once on the stairwell, they glanced carefully over the railing and listened for footsteps. Hearing nothing, they warily moved down a flight of stairs. The access door

to the next floor was locked and had a sign that said
For Maintenance Staff Only, so they descended another level. Still hearing nothing, Jake became convinced that the suspect had left the stairwell and had
reentered the building instead of continuing down the
stairs. He notified the other deputies. Then he and
Dominic stepped through the door, weapons ready.
The lighting in this room was dim. Yet Jake could
tell that he had entered a mailroom of sorts. Piles
of boxes and envelopes littered the tables, and several filing cabinets and sorting bins were arranged
around the room.

Jake carefully surveyed the area and then motioned for Dominic to look toward the right wall.
Despite the insufficient light, he could just make out
the shadow of a man crouching, holding a rifle. Jake
caught Dominic's eye and pointed to himself, indi-
cating his intention to approach the man from behind
and for Dominic to approach from the front. Dominic nodded, and both men slowly and silently started
moving into position so that the shooter would be
trapped between them.

As Jake approached, he could just make out the
sound of Beckett's harried breathing. He felt his own
heart pumping with adrenaline. He took one step and
then another, all the while poised and ready, just in
case the assailant moved or tried to fire on them
again. Finally, he stepped silently around the filing
cabinet behind the man and slowly put the barrel of
his pistol near the man's head.

"Freeze, pal."

Beckett tensed, just as Dominic came into view

from the other direction with his own weapon also pointed at the suspect.

"Now, this is how this is gonna play out," Jake said very succinctly in his leisurely Southern drawl. "You're gonna *very slowly* put your right hand up in the air, and then with your left, you're gonna *very slowly* reach over and put that rifle of yours on the ground. Got it?"

Beckett didn't move, so Jake nudged him with the tip of his pistol. Then Jake noticed that one of Carter's fingers was also inching closer to the trigger. "Move that finger again, buddy, and it will be the last thing you ever do. Got it? I'm done being patient. If you want to leave here in a body bag, that's okay with me."

The man turned his head slightly so he could see Jake's eyes, and something there must have convinced him not to chance it. He slowly raised his right hand and then bent to place the rifle on the floor before raising his left hand, as well.

"Good job. Looks like you can be taught." Kicking the rifle away from Beckett's reach, Jake pushed him against the wall and frisked him. Dominic reached over and picked the rifle up just as Jake pocketed the knife he'd taken out of the man's boot and snapped on the cuffs.

Jake turned Beckett around. He shook his head as he looked the thug in the eye and verified his identity. Finally, this evil man was off the streets. "Carter Beckett. Long time, no see, buddy. Remember us?"

"Yeah," Carter sneered. "You're the guys who keep the doughnut shops in business."

Dominic smiled. "I don't know about that. It's

been…what…about three weeks since I've had a doughnut. Gotta say, though, I love those chocolate-iced ones with the pudding inside. What are those called, Jake?"

"You mean the Boston cream ones?"

Dominic snapped his fingers and pointed at Jake. "That's the one. Man, I love 'em. I might just have to stop by and pick up a dozen after we book this fine gentleman for the long list of crimes he's committed."

Jake returned Dominic's smile, enjoying the banter. "I might do the same myself. I could really go for one with toasted coconut sprinkles on top."

Carter was less than amused. "You guys are pathetic." His tone was bitter.

Jake leaned in close so there was no way Carter would miss his words. "Yet here you are, wearing a pair of my finest bracelets. Your new home is going to be a six-by-six cell at the federal pen, Carter. You have the right to remain silent…"

Shuffling and a clicking noise sounded behind Dominic, and a bright light suddenly flashed on the group. Jake blinked as he also noticed the red light telling him that Mackenzie's video camera was once again filming the scene.

"Ms. Weaver, this is not the time or place…" he growled, using her formal name in front of the criminal in the hopes that she would catch on as to how serious he was about stopping the filming.

She gave him an incredulous look. "Not the time or place? You're kidding, right? What should we be filming if not the arrest of an infamous fugitive?"

"Fugitive?" Beckett said with a laugh, looking directly into the camera. "I'm no fugitive. I'm innocent. I've been framed. This is all a mistake."

Jake tightened his grip on Beckett's arm. "You have the right to be silent, Beckett. I suggest you exercise that right." He met Mackenzie's eyes. They were filled with determination, but he was equally resolute. "Back up, Ms. Weaver, and turn that camera off. We need to get this guy out of here. It'd be nice if we could do it without all the fanfare."

Mackenzie stepped back so the deputies could pass, but the camera remained pointed at them as they moved back toward the stairwell, and the red light never went off.

Jake gritted his teeth and raised the transmitter in his sleeve to his mouth. "We've got the suspect in custody and are heading down. Meet us in the garage."

Once they reached the basement level, Chris Riggs and Whitney Johnson, the other two deputy marshals on the team, approached them and quickly secured Beckett in the back seat of their car.

"Go ahead and take him downtown," Jake directed. He paused a moment, his hands on his hips. "Dominic, why don't we go back up there and take a look at the scene again? I want to check a few things out."

"You got it," Dominic answered. The two men waited for a moment and watched Chris and Whitney drive away. Then they turned back to the stairwell. Mackenzie was still filming, but at least this time she was several yards away.

"The world is a slightly safer place, now that Beckett is off the streets," Dominic said lightly, making sure he spoke softly enough that his words wouldn't be recorded.

Jake laughed. "Amen to that. What I want to know is why all of those broken-down copy machines were in that room. Have you ever seen anything like that?"

"Nope. It's not like this is a repair shop or anything, and there isn't a printing company located here. They had way too many copiers, even for an office building of this size, and there are several different companies here renting out space. They all probably have their own machines, which makes that room of copiers even stranger."

"That's what I'm thinking," Jake agreed. "Something's not right, and I want to know what it is." His instincts were telling him there was more going on here than met the eye, and he always trusted his instincts, even if the clues didn't make any sense at first glance. His gut hadn't failed him yet. He turned and started following Dominic back toward the stairwell as Mackenzie approached them.

"How about an interview, Deputy Marshal?" Mackenzie asked, giving Jake a smile.

Jake turned toward the woman, a mixture of feelings warring within him. Was he angry or just plain scared at the thought of her getting hurt? How could she have taken such unnecessary risks today? She could have gotten shot. She could have gotten killed! Yet she had deliberately put herself in the line of fire, all for the sake of some footage. Maybe she had never grown up after all. He put his hand up in front of the lens. "You could have been critically injured or even killed today. I don't want to see either of those things happen to you. Wasn't being shot at the last two days enough?" He took a step closer. "What we do is dangerous. We don't need bystanders. I told you to stay in the car, and I meant it. You are authorized to do ride-alongs with us. You are not authorized to follow us into buildings as we're pursuing a suspect. Get the picture?" He couldn't keep the anger from his voice.

Mackenzie stiffened her spine and pushed her long brown hair behind her ear. "Look, I'm not thrilled about getting shot at again, but I have to take extreme measures to do my job since you've made it absolutely clear that you aren't going to cooperate. I can't even get you to look at the scripts and storyboards." She turned off her camera and let it drop to her waist. "You've given me no choice, *Deputy Riley*, and I'm well aware of the risks. As you know, I'm actually getting paid to make this documentary, which, I might add, has the approval and support of your district office. Filming you is my job. If I don't work, I don't eat. I can't really make a movie from my desk, now, can I?"

"I'd sure like for you to try."

Mackenzie laughed, and the sweet melodic tone of her voice irritated Jake even more. "What you'd like and what you actually get are two entirely different things, Deputy Marshal."

A muscle tightened in Jake's jaw. He took another step forward, glaring at Mackenzie, but she didn't back down at his intimidating stance. Did this woman have a death wish? What could possibly drive her to take such unnecessary risks? Her positive attitude that had attracted him before was now driving him crazy. "It's probably a really good idea for you to leave now. You need to get back in the car and stay there," he said firmly, his voice filled with menace.

She met his eyes, and Jake could tell she was considering how far to push him. He braced himself for a fight, but none came. A moment passed, then another. Finally, she winked at him, which was the exact opposite of what he expected her to do. A sudden shiver swept over him, and Jake's heart skipped a beat. Why did she have to be so attractive? Her perfume wafted his way again and made him even angrier. She smelled fantastic. He gritted his teeth, frustrated that he was distracted and reacting to her beauty. He didn't want to respond to her in any way. He took a step forward, preparing to blast her once again, but before he could say another word, she took a step back.

"All right, Deputy Marshal. You win. I've got what I came for anyway. I'll pack it in and grab a cab or an Uber back over to the hotel." She pushed a couple of buttons on her camera, and he could hear it powering down. "Thank you for making the arrest. Now that you've captured Beckett, I'm sure the danger is over for me. I'll be perfectly safe from here on out."

Jake wasn't sure that he agreed with her assessment, but he nodded his approval at her decision to leave. Then, as he turned to go back upstairs with Dominic to continue the investigation, a pang of guilt hit him. Was it risky to send her back to the hotel alone? Sure, they had just captured Carter Beckett, the man who had endangered her life in her apartment and probably been behind the shooting, but did that eliminate the threat against her? He refused to analyze the ball of fear that was clenching in his stomach. He knew he cared more than he should, and that line of thought was dangerous, too. He tamped down those feelings deep within him. He didn't want to care about Mackenzie Weaver beyond what he would care for any victim, yet he couldn't seem to stop thinking about her. He opened the stairwell door and turned to watch her for a moment as she stowed her camera equipment. The pain in his stomach intensified. It wasn't a good sign.

God, please help me get this woman out of my system. The silent prayer was quick but heartfelt. He needed help to regain his focus. The desire to pray surprised him, though. It had been a while since he had prayed or attended church. Maybe that was why he'd been struggling so much lately. He ran his hand over his jaw and shook his head. Instead of his worry lightening after the prayer, it seemed to intensify. He instantly knew he couldn't leave her at risk. Maybe God had answered his prayer, but the response was the opposite of what he expected.

He went back over to her side. "Don't call a cab, Ms. Weaver," he growled. "Wait here, and I'll drive you back to the hotel myself. Just give us five minutes to investigate something upstairs. We'll be back shortly. Can you do that?"

Mackenzie shrugged in response and then finally nodded. If today was any indication, this movie was going to be the hardest project she'd ever worked on— all because the deputy marshal she was assigned to work with seemed bent on obstructing her efforts at every turn.

She watched him leave, not trusting herself to speak. She knew on some level that he was right—it had been wrong to follow him into the building, and she had put herself in a risky position. A week ago, she would never even have considered following the deputies into a hot pursuit situation without having more of a plan in place. Yes, she had been afraid of the danger, but for some reason, in her drive to succeed and prove herself, she had convinced herself that the risk was outweighed by the necessity of getting the perfect footage. Now she had to admit that following them hadn't been the smartest move she'd ever made. It had been gratifying to see the man who had pulled a gun on her in her own apartment get arrested, but even that couldn't justify her actions. She had made a mistake. A big one.

She finished packing up her equipment and pulled out her phone, figuring that as long as she had a few minutes to wait, she might as well answer some work-related emails. She tried to focus on the correspondence, but her thoughts kept returning to Jake Riley. Why was the man aggravating her so? It wasn't like she hadn't had difficult clients in the past, but for some reason she couldn't identify, she wanted Jake to like her. No, it was more than that. She wanted Jake to respect her—and the work she did. She wanted his approval. Was she expecting the impossible? He had never seemed to even like her in the past, but that had been years ago, and she was an adult now with totally different dreams and goals. Was she asking too much?

She stowed her phone. She couldn't explain why Jake's opinion mattered so much. It just did. She thought back to her former fiancé, Ted Chapman, whom she had split up with almost a year ago. Ted had loved her but had never really seemed to appreciate her work. In fact, he had always treated her job as a passing hobby rather than a serious profession, just as her parents did. No one except her brother, Jonathan, seemed to truly understand how the movies were a part of her and gave her an ability to express herself on film. And ever since Jonathan's death four years ago, she'd had no one to give her the support she so desperately craved. Mackenzie locked the camera case and closed the trunk, her thoughts spinning. The lighting, the sounds and the framing—they were all a way to give the world meaning and tap into the consciousness of her audience. She wanted to inspire change and encourage people to see things around them in a new and different way. She wanted to stimulate conversations and touch people with her art. Was it even possible to convince Jake to appreciate her efforts?

She sighed. Jake would only be a memory after this film was completed and she'd moved on to her next project. Yet his opinion still mattered to her more than she wanted to admit. Now she just had to figure out why.

She crossed her arms and clenched her fists in frustration. Had she just blown this opportunity by her thoughtless actions?

SIX

"I don't want Mackenzie Weaver anywhere near my team," Jake said emphatically. "She's out of control, and she's going to get herself killed."

Jake's supervisor, J.T. Austin, leaned back in his chair. "Look, Jake. I understand how you feel, but this assignment came from the assistant director himself. We have to let Weaver do ride-alongs and cover us in the field, at least until this documentary she's working on is complete. We have no choice in the matter."

"That's ridiculous. She's a liability out there, and if we're not careful, she's going to end up in the line of fire. She almost got shot yesterday during the Beckett arrest. Can't we send her up to Atlanta or one of the larger offices? Maybe they can babysit her."

"No can do," J.T. said quietly. "You have to understand the political background here. Funding is tight for all federal agencies, and the US Marshals units have been getting the short end of the stick at appropriations time lately, especially the smaller units like ours. This documentary is going to show everyone how important our job really is and make sure we get the funding we need to do it correctly."

Jake steamed. He had never been good at playing the political game. "How's it going to sound on the evening news when Ms. Weaver gets shot by friendly fire? I'm telling you, she has no business being out there. She doesn't understand how law enforcement works."

"Didn't you brief her before you went out for the arrest? What she could and couldn't do should have been spelled out to her."

"Oh, it was spelled out all right," Jake said roughly. "She was told to stay behind the perimeter and in the car until the arrest was completed. She just didn't do what she was told."

J.T. rubbed his chin. "Are you upset because she broke the rules or because you don't want her out there in the first place?"

Jake ran his hands through his hair. "Both. She's new at this, but she just needs somebody to teach her some basic safety procedures. The problem is, she's reckless. I'm sure she's never touched a weapon in her entire life and probably doesn't realize the danger, even though she's been shot at repeatedly over the last few days. She seems to just keep coming back for more. She's either the gutsiest woman I've ever met or the most naive lady on the planet."

"You have a point. What she needs is someone to help her get to know the ropes so she can be an asset to your team, rather than a hindrance. Thanks for volunteering, Jake," J.T. said with a smile. "It will ease my mind knowing you've taken this project on."

Jake raised his eyebrows and sat down heavily. "Wow. I didn't see that coming."

J.T. leaned forward. "Look, Jake, like it or not, we're stuck with her, and the faster she gets the job done, the faster she's out of our hair. Think of it this way. By helping her out, you'll be helping yourself." He paused. "Is the threat against her neutralized now that Beckett has been arrested?"

"I don't know. We're still trying to connect all the dots."

"Until you know for sure, she's probably safer in your company than she would be out on her own. In the grand scheme of things, you're actually helping out a victim by keeping her close. Isn't that why you joined the US Marshals in the first place? To protect people?"

Jake closed his eyes for a moment and blew out a breath. Ever since Beckett's arrest yesterday, he had been avoiding Mackenzie to the best of his ability. He'd had Dominic take her back to her hotel after they'd finished searching the office building, and today he'd done a quick disappearing act whenever she was nearby. He definitely did not relish the idea of spending time with her. He'd even spent hours trying to interrogate Beckett this morning—and gotten absolutely nowhere—just so he wouldn't run into Mackenzie in the bull pen.

He glanced over at his boss, who had tented his fingers and was waiting patiently for him to sort through his thoughts. Unfortunately, Jake knew that further argument wouldn't alter the situation. J.T. Austin was a fair-minded and supportive supervisor, but he could also rarely be talked into changing his mind once it was made up.

"Okay. Fine. I'll try to work something out with her," Jake mumbled. He shifted in his chair and decided to change the subject before he showed J.T. just how much Mackenzie had gotten under his skin. "You'll see in my report the details of the Beckett arrest and his interrogation, but we came across something strange that we haven't been able to figure out."

J.T. raised an eyebrow. "What's that?"

"A whole room dedicated to taking apart copy machines. Dozens and dozens of them. The office building doesn't house a repair shop, so it was really odd. I'm not sure what to make of it."

"Where did the machines come from?"

"A variety of sources. We started a trace based on their serial numbers, and found that most of them were purchased from an auction a few weeks ago. Some used to belong to a variety of state agencies, and others to medical offices. The purchases are legitimate, but what we can't figure out is why that company, or any company really, would need so many. Do you have any ideas?"

"None," J.T. said, shaking his head. "Is it really that big of a deal? So they have a collection of copy machines. So what?"

Jake shrugged. "I don't know. It may mean nothing at all. It's just my gut talking. Something seems wrong about the whole thing."

"Don't spend too much time on it if it doesn't pan out. We've got too many other cases in the hopper."

Jake stood, nodded to his boss, and went in search

of his new protégé. He knew she was in the building somewhere. The agency had given her a temporary desk for the duration of her project, but he was surprised when he actually saw her sitting there, tapping away on her computer. All morning and afternoon she had seemed to be up and about, asking questions or getting underfoot in some other annoying way. He had even seen her filming in one of the spare conference rooms that morning. Apparently, she had found a few willing participants and had been interviewing them on camera. The fact that he'd noticed her behavior and had been keeping tabs on her annoyed him even further.

He stopped a moment before approaching her and really looked at her. She was definitely quite attractive, with high cheekbones and a full, wide mouth that was usually smiling. Her cheerfulness irritated him, as did the fact that he couldn't take his eyes off her. He noticed how her chocolate-brown hair softly framed her face, and her pale blue eyes were warm and expressive. He drew his lips into a thin line. Attractive or not, she had no business being in his workplace. He wondered just how long it would take before he would be free of her and her interference.

Mackenzie put a stray strand of hair behind her ear and pushed some more keys on her laptop. The editing software she had installed on her computer was top of the line, but it was nothing like the professional version she'd had to work with back at her home studio. The insurance company was slowly working on her claim, but it would be a while before she could replace her equipment and do the professional editing necessary to fulfill her commitments. In the meantime, she was trying to make arrangements to rent out another company's editing board so she could finish the video on the homeless by her deadline. She made a few clicks on her keyboard, taking another look at her footage from the Beckett arrest. Even though the software wasn't the best, it still gave her an idea of what footage she had and what she still needed to record to complete the project at hand. She grimaced and hit the delete button, erasing a section of the film. There was virtually nothing usable from yesterday's shoot at the arrest, and every time she got to the part with Deputy Riley's hand in front of the lens, it made her fume.

"Playing video games again?"

The smooth Southern drawl startled her. She jumped and looked up into Jake's face. She had been so engrossed in her work that she hadn't even noticed him approach.

Her first reaction was to vent her frustration at his interference, but she smiled at him instead. There was no use making a bad situation worse, and if she antagonized him, her job would get even harder, not to mention the fact that she still needed to apologize for her own behavior yesterday during the arrest. As hard as it was to admit, she had been wrong and needed to tell him so. She motioned toward a nearby chair, inviting him to sit. "Actually, I have the Pac-Man high score. Some of those retro games are pretty cool."

He raised an eyebrow and then pulled up the chair and sat down in front of her. "You probably remember that I'm an up-front kind of guy. I'm not good at word games or sugarcoating things, so let me just say this straight up. You're dangerous. You're gonna make a mistake and land right in my sights if you're not careful, and you're gonna get hurt. When we go out on an arrest, we have one primary objective, and that is to capture our target. We use real guns with real bullets. If you get in the way again like you did yesterday, we can't stop what we're doing to move you out of the way. You'll end up being collateral damage. You could get killed."

Mackenzie closed her laptop with a snap. "Look, I realize I made a mistake yesterday, and I'm sorry."

Jake didn't respond, so she pushed forward. "I do have a job to do, though, and a deadline to meet. If you don't cooperate from here on out, I'll get way behind with the shooting schedule and won't be able to fulfill my contract deliverables. Not to mention the fact that the US Marshals office in Atlanta sanctioned this project and promised me full cooperation."

Jake held up his hands. "True. I was just reminded of that fact. I was also just assigned to be your babysitter."

Mackenzie narrowed her eyes. "Babysitter? I don't think so. I'm almost twenty-seven years old. I can handle myself just fine."

"Apparently you can't follow directions. Don't you remember your instructions during the briefing yesterday before the arrest? You were supposed to stay behind the perimeter and in the car until we had Beckett in custody. Instead, you went barging in before we had even cleared the floor."

Mackenzie drew her lips into a thin line. As much as she hated to admit it to him, she knew he had a point. Unfortunately, her actions had probably destroyed the minuscule amount of goodwill he'd ever harbored for her and her project. "You're right, and I apologize again. If it helps, I'll say I'm sorry a third time. If you would cooperate, though, it would save me from having to go to such extreme measures in the future to get this documentary finished."

Jake's eyes widened. "Are you saying this is my fault?"

Mackenzie nodded her head. "Partly, yes. I was wrong to follow you. I already admitted that. I realize now my behavior was a serious mistake. I shouldn't have done that. But unfortunately, I'll probably have to do something risky again if you won't support this project. Put yourself in my shoes. What would you do to get your job accomplished if someone blocked you at every turn? Would you let a suspect escape just because you had an uncooperative witness? I've seen you in action and know you're good at your job. Very good. And I'm sure you'd do whatever it takes to get the job done. I'm the same way, even if my job is different. I'm committed to this, and this work is just as important to me as yours is to you. When I'm finished, it will have my name on it, and I won't submit sloppy work."

Jake looked as if he was actually considering her words. He let a moment pass, then another. Finally, he spoke. "Touché. I haven't made a secret of the fact that I don't think we need a documentary, and I guess I haven't been very helpful."

Mackenzie raised an eyebrow. Had he just admitted his lack of cooperation? She watched as he leaned back in the chair, his expression thoughtful.

"Why don't you tell me again what you want? Then maybe we can work something out. I have no idea what happened to that script you gave me."

Mackenzie blinked. Had he just agreed to help her? That was not the response she had expected. Ever since they'd met as teenagers, he had been trying to get rid of her. She hadn't expected to make any actual headway. She switched gears. "Okay, fine. I'll get you another copy of the script and the storyboard, and you can start by looking those over and giving me your comments. I've already finished the general background research on the US Marshals unit here and gotten some basic shots that lead the viewer through the fundamentals, but what I really want is to take the audience through one of your typical cases, you know, from start to finish, to give them a feel for what you do. Then I want to get some shots of you guys in action. There wasn't much from yesterday's shoot that was usable."

Jake crossed his arms. "Okay. Let's talk this through. If I agree to let you document us working a case, will you follow my directions *explicitly* and stay out of the way when I tell you to? I'm not trying to be a jerk about this. I just really don't want to see you get hurt."

Mackenzie wasn't so sure she believed him since they'd had a similar conversation when she had first arrived, but this olive branch he was extending seemed to be the only way she might actually be able to finish her movie. It was a start. If his boss had assigned him to babysit her, maybe he had also convinced him to help her. "Done, but I need to be kept in the loop. You can't rush out of the office for a bust and not expect me to follow you."

Jake paused a moment and then put out his hand. "You've got a deal."

Mackenzie shook his hand but quickly dropped it as she felt electricity shoot up her arm. She looked up at Jake, who had a strange look in his eyes. They were the greenest eyes she had ever seen, and they reminded her of a stained glass window on a bright summer day. Funny. She hadn't even noticed how incredibly clear they were until this very moment. Even some of the sadness she had seen before seemed to have dissipated and been replaced with an intensity that she couldn't quite identify. She leaned back, uncomfortable with where her thoughts were leading her. Even though she had broken up with Ted over a year ago, the pain from losing him had been tough to bear. She was in no hurry to start up a new relationship with anyone, especially not with the troubling man before her. That thought actually made her want to laugh. She was pretty sure that Jake didn't even like her— and never had. The mere idea of having a relationship with him was preposterous. The best she could hope for was that he would put up with her until this project was over. Earning his approval for her work seemed like an utterly impossible task.

She pushed her negative thoughts aside. "Okay. Where do we start?" she asked, wiping her hands on her jeans.

Jake raised an eyebrow. "Are you ready to roll up your sleeves?"

"Absolutely."

"Good." He handed her a piece of paper from a folder he had brought over with him. "You've probably already realized our work isn't always action-packed. A large part of what we do is research. This is a list of the serial numbers from the copy machines we found yesterday during Beckett's arrest. Some came from medical offices, and some from state agencies. I need you to find out how they all got in that building, and why anyone would want or need that many in the first place. It may not lead to anything, but Dominic and I just didn't feel right about what we found there. Sometimes odd things need a second look. I want you to research it and find out what you can, and give me a theory or two to explain it. If you follow this lead and it actually takes you somewhere, you can follow us along to film it when it pans out."

"And if it doesn't? I don't mind doing some leg-work, but if you're just keeping me busy to get me out of the way…"

Jake shook his head. "This is legitimate. In fact, I would normally do it myself. I've just got a lot on my plate right now, and you will actually be helping me out."

Again, Mackenzie wasn't convinced of his sincerity, but there was no use looking for problems if there weren't any. She glanced at the paper and saw a list of almost forty machines.

"That office had this many copy machines?"

"Yep. All in various states of disrepair."

"All right. I'll check this out."

Jake nodded. "Good. Come find me if you discover anything." His phone buzzed and he answered, his brow furrowing as he spoke to the caller in short, one- and two-word responses. Finally, he hung up and met her eye.

"We've got a problem. Your hotel room was just ransacked, and the maid apparently interrupted the crime and was shot."

Fear jolted through Mackenzie's heart. "Was she killed?"

"No, they've rushed her to the hospital. She's in critical condition, but they think she'll pull through." He put his hands on his hips. "We're still missing something here. Even with Carter Beckett out of the picture, you're in danger. And he's not talking. He lawyered up as soon as we tried to interview him. We're going to have to put you into protective custody until we figure this out."

A sliver of dread swept down Mackenzie's spine, and she said a silent prayer for the maid. She had assumed the threat had been neutralized with Beckett's capture. After all, they had already found the link between her street children movie and Beckett's location. Why was someone still trying to hurt her?

SEVEN

Mackenzie eyed the beautiful country landscape as she and Jake drove slowly down the dirt road. Large live oak trees dotted the rolling hills, and someone had planted along the easement a row of pink crepe myrtle trees that were in full, glorious bloom. She checked the side-view mirror once more, verifying that nobody was following them, just as they turned right by a rusty metal mailbox. Despite the attractive setting, her stomach was twisting in knots. The notion that someone was still trying to kill her terrified her. The fact that others were getting hurt because of her made the entire situation even worse.

"Don't worry. Nobody is tailing us," Jake said softly. His Southern inflection was somewhat comforting, but Mackenzie couldn't seem to make her apprehension melt away. They had spent over an hour at the hotel going through the ransacked room, but even so, it didn't appear that anything was missing. The entire situation was an enigma; she just couldn't figure out why someone would want to hurt her or go through her things.

She was worried about the threat against her, but now she also felt like an incredible burden. Jake and the other deputies had searched for a safe house that they could use to protect her, but to no avail. Jake had eventually volunteered to put her up at his house since it was off the beaten trail, but Mackenzie could tell that his offer was solely based on his professionalism and work ethic, and she had heard the reluctance in his voice when he volunteered. He had assured her that he lived alone and she was welcome there and wasn't inconveniencing anyone, but Mackenzie didn't like being an encumbrance, especially to Jake, whose relationship with her was already tenuous at best.

She glanced in his direction and watched him maneuver the road with ease. Ever since she met Jake Riley all those years ago, Mackenzie had sensed and noted his acute perception. He seemed to be able to see straight inside of her and read her mind and heart with a simple gaze. She didn't have the same ability, however, and she wondered what he was thinking.

The dirt driveway made several twists and turns before ending at a small redbrick house. The home had a modern design and looked oddly out of place in the bucolic setting. Behind the house was a large barn, and much of the yard was fenced off for pasture that stretched out on all sides of the homestead. Azaleas and hydrangea bushes flanked the front of the house, and a large pecan tree graced the front yard. It was a peaceful milieu, but Mackenzie felt anything but peaceful as she grabbed her small bag of toiletries and clothing that had been salvaged from the hotel and followed Jake inside the house.

He gave her a quick tour and then showed her the guest bedroom. "You'll be in here. The other deputies will be arriving shortly, and we'll all take turns keeping an eye on things." He handed her a small gray bag. "Here's your cell phone and the battery. Don't put the battery back in your regular phone until this whole event is over. Even if the phone isn't turned on, if it has the battery in it, you can be tracked." He handed her a second phone. "This is a secure phone that can't be tracked. Use it for now, and you can give it back once it's safe to go back to your old phone. Deal?"

Mackenzie nodded, pleased that he had made arrangements for her to have some way to communicate with the outside world during her sequestration.

"Ever had any firearm training?"

She shook her head. "No. I've never even held a gun."

"That ends today. I have a small range set up behind the barn."

He must have been able to see the uncertainty on her face because he raised an eyebrow. "Is there a problem?"

She shrugged. "No, I guess not." She absently ran her hand along the edge of the dresser. "I have to admit I feel a little awkward being here."

"Why?"

"I guess because I know that you really don't want to be doing this, and I feel like I'm invading your privacy. You've never wanted me around."

He smiled at her, and the smile did funny things to her insides. "Honesty. I like that. I like the way you speak your mind. I don't have to wonder what you're thinking."

Mackenzie laughed, noting that he hadn't disagreed with her assessment. "Really? I've always thought it was one of my biggest faults. With some people, honesty can be the last thing they want to hear."

"Well, I'm not one of them. I guess it's because I hear so many lies from the people we chase that I find the truth refreshing." Jake leaned casually against the door frame. "I'll pay you the compliment of being honest with you right back. The truth is I think everyone should know how to defend themselves, so I really don't mind spending my time teaching you. And as for you staying at my place, I wouldn't have invited you out if I didn't want you here. Sure, it wasn't my first choice, but I do want to keep you safe. I'll do whatever it takes to protect you." He gave her another smile, and Mackenzie noted these were some of the first smiles she'd seen him offer. This was a different side of Jake that she hadn't seen for quite a while. He was relaxed, and although she wouldn't quite call him happy, he was definitely less intense than he had been the last couple of days. It was intriguing.

He ran his hands through his hair. "I was a dumb kid back in college. Jonathan and I, well, we weren't the most considerate guys on the planet, and we didn't treat you very well. I'm sorry for that." He tilted his head a bit and nodded toward the back of his house. "Let's forget the past and start fresh. I'd love it if you let me show you my horses before your visit is over. I'm actually quite proud of them."

He motioned to the house in general and pushed away from the door frame. "Please make yourself at home." He turned and left her to settle in.

For a moment she just sat on the bed, thinking through their conversation. Had he really just apologized for the way he had acted when she was in high school? It was the first time he had actually mentioned something about their shared history in a positive light. Just like her mistakes during the arrest, she had to admit, the hurts she had sustained in the past weren't all his fault. She had been a pain to both Jake and her brother and had gone overboard on more than one occasion when she'd been trying to get their attention. Maybe it really was time to put the past behind them.

Dear God, please help us heal this relationship. Help us both work through our issues so we can get our jobs done. Thank You for giving us both a second opportunity to make things right, and thank You for keeping me safe.

Sighing, she stood and opened the closet. She admired the room as she hung up a shirt. It was well lit, with plenty of sunshine coming through the windows, and was sparsely but tastefully decorated.

She finished unpacking and sat down at the small desk in the corner. Opening her laptop, she signed on to Jake's Wi-Fi network with the new login Jake had given her. She was strong and confident in her abilities. Maybe if she kept her focus on her current project for the US Marshals, she could keep her mind away from her own troubles. She had always handled her own problems in the past, and this death threat would not be the exception.

She tapped a few keys and took a deep breath, focusing on the job at hand. She had been warned to stay away from her email and other sites where she could be tracked to her current location, but she had been given the go-ahead to do basic research. She started with a search of the businesses in the building where the copy machines had been found but didn't find any company that would need that many machines. Then she did a general search of businesses that did use a large number of copiers, but couldn't find any matches between those and the ones currently housed in the building, either. So who would want or need so many of them?

She heard the other deputies arrive but stayed in the room doing her investigation. A couple of hours later, her head was still reeling from what she had discovered. She finally went in search of Jake and found him bent over his own keyboard, sitting at his desk in a corner of the living room. His forehead was wrinkled and it was obvious from his stance that he had been sitting there for quite some time. The other deputies were nowhere to be seen.

"Ready for a break? I've got some info I want to run by you."

Jake leaned back and rubbed his forehead. "Absolutely. If I sit here much longer, I'm just going to whip out my weapon and shoot this stupid computer."

"Having trouble? Maybe I can help." She leaned over to look at his screen, and her hair brushed his arm. He pulled back to get out of her way, and again she noticed an odd look on his face.

"No problem. I know my way around a computer, but I sure hate the paperwork. It's absolutely the worst part of the job. I'm several days behind, so I've spent the last few hours playing catch-up." He cleared his throat. "Why don't you have a seat and tell me what you discovered. Like I said, I can really use the break." He motioned toward a chair by his desk and she took it, pushing a lock of hair behind her ear.

"All right, here's the scoop. Around 2002, the copy machine manufacturers joined the modern age and started putting hard drives in their machines, just like the one in your laptop there. Some copiers even have two hard drives inside. The hard drives store an image of every document that gets copied, emailed or scanned, and they rarely get erased, if ever. The machines in question were previously leased by several agencies—two law firms, a mortgage company, the downtown library, the Florida Department of Corrections and Department of Highway Safety, and three medical offices. Each copier was then sold at auction for about five hundred dollars. Apparently, that's how the copier company gets rid of old inventory before rolling in the newest technology. No one keeps track of who buys them, how many they purchase or why, beyond the usual sales receipts." She paused and handed him the list. "Now, here's my theory. Step one—you take the hard drive out of the old copy machine. I figure it takes thirty minutes to an hour to do it, unless you're a skilled technician. I even found a YouTube video that explains how to do it. Step two—download this program I got for free on the internet, run a scan on the hard drive and download all the saved documents. I figure that could take a while, depending on the speed of your computer, because we're talking thousands of documents, not just a few hundred. Step three—sort through them all for the info you want, discard the trash and, voilà, you've got access to all kinds of private information such as social security numbers, bank records, income tax forms, medical records, etc. without anyone being the wiser. You get the picture. And considering that some of these machines came from Highway Safety, you might also have driver's license numbers and photos. Step four—you're ready for identity theft."

Jake stood abruptly. His gut had been right, but this was even bigger than he'd imagined. Much bigger. "Hold that thought. I want to get the whole team in here to hear what you're saying. Let me gather them up, and we'll do an impromptu meeting right here in the living room." He met her eye. "You did well, Mackenzie. I mean it."

"Wow. That must've hurt." Mackenzie raised an eyebrow and gave him a smile.

Jake could tell his praise had pleased her. He nodded at her and motioned to his couch before going in search of his team members, who were doing a perimeter walk around the property.

A few minutes later, Mackenzie repeated her findings to Dominic, Whitney and Chris, the other three deputy marshals on Jake's team.

Dominic whistled as she finished describing her

discovery. "You know, if anyone gets hold of those medical records alone, we're talking a serious breach of federal privacy law. This is really big. Identity theft is one thing, but why stop there? It's a perfect storm for extortion, too."

Whitney nodded in agreement. "This is something I never even considered. I mean, who knew that copy machines stored all that data? I sure didn't. I just figured the machines made copies. I didn't know they stockpiled the images after the fact."

"I didn't, either," Chris agreed. "And think of all those people who use the copier in the library. Who knows what kind of personal information is stored in that machine? There could be tax returns, business documents, all kinds of things. The sky is the limit. And now most machines handle faxes and scans, too, so whoever gets the hard drives can access all sorts of private records."

Jake stood. "Look, I know everyone has a lot going on, but we need to move on this case right now before those copy machines disappear. So far, we have an excellent theory, but no real proof of wrongdoing. After all, it's not illegal to buy or own used copy machines. We have to figure out how these tie in to Beckett's criminal acts so we can stop this before it goes any further." He glanced over at Dominic. "Did Beckett ever break down and talk?"

Dominic shook his head. "Nope. Local police took a run at him too, but after a few minutes of saying nothing, he asked for a lawyer and clammed up again. We're not going to get anything out of him."

Jake drew his lips into a straight line as he ab-

sorbed the information and then motioned to Mackenzie. "I promised Mackenzie that she could film
us for her documentary as we progress on the case.
You'll be seeing her with her camera quite a bit." He
paused and looked around the table. "Whitney, find
out all you can about Allied Incorporated. That's the
parent company that bought the machines according
to the invoices, and it's the same company that seems
to be storing them at that building where we arrested
Beckett. Chris, you and Dominic find out if Beckett
has any ties to Allied. Mackenzie, what do you need
for your movie?"

Mackenzie stood, as well. "I'd like to set up in here
and film your next meeting when you come back with
what you've all learned. I'll be careful during the editing process to make sure no actual names are mentioned of the suspects, but I want to show you meeting
and collaborating. Will that work? We can even do a
narration over the video if you're worried about the
audio leaking valuable information."

Jake knew that a look of discomfort had probably
just swept across his face, but he finally nodded. "All
right. It's getting late. Let's meet back here tomorrow
morning at nine with whatever you've got."

He glanced at Mackenzie, whose cheeks were a
vibrant pink. He could see the excitement in her eyes
as well and knew that her success and his cooperation
had put it there. He liked the feeling. He also had to
admit that her research had paid off. Now they had a
real lead into Beckett's criminal enterprise. He didn't
know where it would take them, but he had a feeling
they'd only scratched the surface. No wonder Beckett

was intent on silencing Mackenzie and destroying her movie. If he hadn't seen the video on homeless children that she had made, he would never have made the connection and found the copy machines in the first place. It could be the tip of the iceberg on a much larger criminal enterprise.

The next morning, the team reassembled around Jake's coffee table. Mackenzie turned on the bright light and pointed it in his direction. Jake blinked. "Is that really necessary?"

"It is," Mackenzie answered as she stepped carefully around the tripod. "Lighting is everything. Without that light, you'd be surprised where the shadows end up."

He squinted and pushed back in his chair. He could come up with at least ten other places he'd rather be at this moment—maybe fifteen. He'd never even liked getting his picture taken, so being in a video made him acutely uncomfortable. Still, he had made a promise. "All right, let's get this over with. We can film it once and be done, right?"

"Right," Mackenzie responded. She looked around at the deputies. "I'm ready when you are."

Whitney passed around a small packet of papers to everyone and started speaking. "Okay. Here's what we know about Allied Incorporated. It's a small title insurance company with connections to several real estate brokers and law firms here in Tallahassee. They rent that floor where the copiers were found and two other rooms that they apparently use as offices. The building has four other companies renting space, by the way, but none of them seem to have any ties to Allied. Anyway, three guesses as to who the president of Allied is." Mackenzie looked around the room, but nobody ventured a guess. "Come on, guys. Think loan fraud," Whitney added.

"Derek Lager," Jake said suddenly, as the name popped into his head.

"Give that man a prize," Whitney said. "Derek Lager is apparently back in business."

Dominic shook his head. "We're going to have to call the FBI."

Jake nodded. "Yeah. Just what I wanted to do today." In the past, Jake hadn't minded working with the FBI, but ever since Chuck Holiday, a rogue FBI agent, had tried to kill a witness whom Jake and his team had been protecting, the thought of working with the FBI left a bitter taste in his mouth. Chuck had gone through a messy divorce and had a slew of financial problems, but in Jake's mind, nothing justified attempted murder. The witness had ended up with a bullet in the lung, but one good thing had come out of the situation—Dominic had married that witness, and they were very happy together.

"What else do you have?" Jake asked Whitney.

"I haven't found out who Lager's working with this time around, but I'm chasing down some leads."

Jake turned to Dominic. "What did you and Chris find out?"

"If there's a connection between Beckett and Allied, or Beckett and Lager, we haven't found it." Dominic answered. "At least not yet."

"It could be that Beckett had other business in the

building that wasn't tied to the copiers," Chris added. "Maybe it was just a coincidence that you discovered those copy machines during the arrest."

Jake nodded. "Could be. Beckett's never had any fraud or identity theft on his rap sheet, but there still might be some sort of connection since he was in front of that building in Mackenzie's movie and was back when we searched the building. He had some reason for being there on a regular basis. We need to find out why." He turned back to Whitney. "Looks like our next move is to do some research on Beckett and then find Lager and do some surveillance. Any ideas where to start?"

"I've already put out some feelers about Lager, but haven't heard anything back yet," Whitney confirmed.

Jake looked up at Mackenzie, who gave him the thumbs-up sign. He was silently thankful that she had gotten what she wanted in only one take and they could turn the camera off. Authorized or not, he didn't think he would ever feel comfortable in front of the camera. He turned his thoughts back to the case at hand. "All right. You know what to do. Let's do it." Once a suspect was identified, each member of the team had certain duties that they had all done several times before such as searching various databases, applying for warrants and other research. Everyone knew that time was of the essence, and they dispersed, heading off to perform their duties. They had to begin by developing enough probable cause to seize the copy machines before Derek Lager and the evidence disappeared forever.

EIGHT

A few moments later, Mackenzie and Jake were alone in the room.

"Who is Derek Lager?" she asked, taking a chair across from Jake.

"A criminal we've had our eyes on for a couple of years now. He's got a lengthy rap sheet. Our team first got introduced to him when he jumped bail a few years ago in an interstate mortgage fraud case. We caught up to him over near Panama City and got him back in custody, but even though it was incredibly obvious that he was guilty, the legal case against him fell apart at the last minute. He only ended up spending a few months in jail for some minor charges. He's the best forger I've ever seen."

"Does he counterfeit money?"

"Nah. Lager's thing is driver's licenses, which is of particular interest since some of those machines you researched came from Highway Safety. I'm sure he's in business again. The only question is what he's using the fake licenses for this time. I think you had the right idea when you mentioned identity theft."

Mackenzie gave him a smile. "So when do you want to show me your horses?"

"Once the threat against you is neutralized, we'll be sure to take a walk through my barn." He tilted his head. "Do you ride?"

"I've always thought horses were beautiful, but I've never actually been on one before. To be honest, the thought is kind of scary to me. They're pretty big animals."

Jake laughed and put up his hands. "What? Hold up a minute. You mean you'll go charging into a building where bullets are flying, but you're afraid of riding a horse?"

Mackenzie shrugged. "Yep, that about sums it up."

Jake shook his head. "Riding a horse is the best thing out there. If you ever get an opportunity to do it, you should."

"I'll keep that in mind." She rose to leave, but Jake motioned for her to sit back down.

He wasn't relishing the upcoming conversation, but it had to happen sooner or later. "Look, I need to teach you a few things so you don't end up getting shot the next time we're out in the field."

Mackenzie crossed her arms. "I already told you that I don't need a babysitter."

"I know. I was thinking more along the lines of some basic safety training."

Mackenzie let her arms drop, and her stance was slightly less confrontational. "Like what?"

"The firearms training I mentioned before is the best place to start, but there's more to it than that."

"If that's what you think, I trust your judgment,

but I can't imagine that I'll ever actually use a gun while I'm with you…"

"You might not have to," Jake interrupted, "but if you do, I want you to know something about the weapon so you'll have an idea of how it works. You'll also have a better idea of what we do if you are familiar with the tools we use. There are some other basic things I'd like to go over with you, just so you'll be safer out in the field the next time around."

He noticed Mackenzie's glance at the shelves near his desk where he displayed the sharpshooter medals, trophies and plaques that he'd won over the years in various shooting contests. She didn't look all that impressed, but to him, the assortment of awards represented one of the most successful aspects of his life. He had always enjoyed working with guns and was an incredibly talented marksman. When the agency needed someone to take a difficult shot, it was Jake they called.

She turned back to face him, still not looking all that thrilled with the idea, but in the end, she finally agreed. "All right. When?"

"How about now?" Jake was hesitant to spend more time with her, but at the same time, he felt a wave of protectiveness sweep over him whenever he looked in her direction. Mackenzie Weaver was in danger, and he wanted to do whatever it took to keep her safe. There was something odd about the way she made him feel—something that kept him off balance and drew him to her like a moth to a flame. His work left little time for socializing, and that was the way he liked it. Also, he wasn't convinced there were too many decent people left in the world outside of the team he worked with at the US Marshals. Still, thoughts of Mackenzie swept through his mind at the oddest times, despite his resolve to remain alone. What he needed was distance, and that wasn't going to happen until this movie of hers was finished and they neutralized the threat against her.

Jake led Mackenzie into his kitchen then removed a 9 mm Beretta from a drawer by the sink. He took out the clip and handed her the weapon.

"Wow, it's heavier than it looks," Mackenzie said, her voice revealing her surprise.

"That's a common reaction. It weighs about two and a half pounds fully loaded. Now, first things first. Never, and I mean never, point a weapon at someone unless you intend to use it, even if you know that the weapon is empty. Second rule—keep your finger off the trigger until you're ready to shoot." He made a motion with his hands. "This is a semiautomatic double-action pistol. It holds fifteen rounds fully loaded. You put the bullets in this clip, and once you insert the clip, you're ready to go." He showed her the bullets but didn't insert them. Then he slid the empty clip into the weapon. "Most guns have a safety, so if you're not going to be shooting the gun right away, you need to keep the safety on." He showed her where the safety lever was and the red dot that appeared when the weapon was ready to fire. Then he showed her the button to push to release the clip.

"Is this your service weapon?"

Jake shook his head. "No. We carry a Glock 22 on the job, but I was introduced to the Beretta by a friend from the army, and I always liked them. This is my personal weapon."

Mackenzie raised an eyebrow. "Was it Jonathan?"

He heard a touch of pain in her voice. "No, a different friend. But Jonathan and I did like to shoot together. That's one of the places we would run off to when we were in college."

"Really?" she asked as she handled the gun and released the clip. "Where else would you go?"

He smiled. "Other places where younger kid sisters would get in the way." She didn't look up, so he pushed on. "Look, I know for a fact that Jonathan loved you. I'm sure of it. But you have to understand, we were in college and you were in high school. We were living a different kind of lifestyle, and unfortunately, we were a tad on the selfish side."

"And you didn't have time for a bratty kid sister tagging along. I do understand now that I'm older. Believe me. And I have to admit I could be a pain sometimes. It's just that now that he's gone, I miss him more than ever, and I wish I had that time back, you know?" She shook her head, as if shaking off the melancholy. "Hey, didn't we agree to leave the past in the past? Let's go do some target practice." She handed him back the weapon and stood, apparently ready for the next step.

Jake took the gun from her, slid the clip out of the weapon and loaded it, checked the safety and then motioned for the door. He noticed that she'd changed the subject, but he didn't push. "Shall we?"

She followed him out the door and around the side of his barn. On the far end he had a huge mound of dirt as a backstop, and several targets of various sizes and colors set up. At the other end he had a small table that had several boxes of bullets and two sets of ear protectors. He used his phone to text the other deputies and notify them of their plans and then turned to her.

"Ready to give it a try?"

She looked up at him and seemed to be a bit self-conscious. "Tell me again why you think this is necessary?"

"This is just a part of the lesson," he reassured her. "I want you to have a good understanding of what we do. I can't teach you everything in a few hours, of course, but I want you to know the basics so if something goes wrong out there, you'll have at least a possibility of getting out alive." He handed her the ear protectors. "I can't stress enough how dangerous this job is."

She nodded, then put on the ear protectors and took the weapon when he handed it to her. She watched closely as he showed her how to slide the top of the weapon to insert a bullet into the chamber and how to aim the gun properly.

"Okay. See the green target? Aim for the bull's-eye, and let's see how you do."

She pushed off the safety lever and wrapped her finger around the trigger. Her first shot went wild, as did her second shot. She looked over at him and raised an eyebrow. "I guess this is harder than it looks."

Jake smiled. "Don't worry. It takes a while to get the hang of it. Remember to squeeze the trigger gently. Don't jerk or pull it." He got closer and repositioned her hands, making sure she was supporting the weapon correctly. He was so close that he could smell her perfume and her hair tickled his cheek. He took a step back, unhappy with the thoughts that were suddenly swimming in his head. He did *not* need to be attracted to this woman, even if she did smell like sunshine and looked absolutely amazing, although just in her simple jeans and Florida State University T-shirt. *Focus*, he chided himself silently. *Keep your eye on the ball here.*

She took another shot that also went wild, and before he even thought about it, Jake was behind her, his arms wrapped around her and supporting her hands. "This time, *squeeze* the trigger slowly, and don't close your eyes. You're still jerking the trigger just a little bit." He tensed, trying to ignore how comfortable and sweet she felt in his arms. He didn't want to be attracted to her. He didn't want to be attracted to anyone. On the job, he had run across such monstrous and repulsive behavior that it was hard to imagine that inner beauty still existed. Still, there was something about Mackenzie…

He thought back to the case that had crushed his spirit. About six months ago, a father on their most-wanted list had viciously murdered his two young children and then turned the gun on himself, rather than be arrested and face a return to prison. The more they had investigated the case, the more they discovered the incredible abuse and cruelty the children had been forced to endure. Watching the coroner zip the body bags on those two kids had almost been his undoing, and ever since then, his heart had hardened like a stone. The US Marshals had offered counseling, and he'd participated, but even that hadn't been enough to erase the pain he felt. He had turned to God and found a measure of relief, but then he had slowly stopped praying and had been basically trying to handle everything on his own. Now he was coming to realize that his actions had been a mistake. He was definitely still a work in progress. He needed God in his life. When he had prayed about Mackenzie, it had been like a breath of fresh air to his soul. God was using Mackenzie in many ways to affect him.

She fired again, and his focus returned to his firearms lesson. This time, he could make out the hole on the target just shy of the bull's-eye. He turned so he could see Mackenzie's face, and their eyes locked. She looked both pleased and nervous at the same time. Had he ever seen eyes that color? They were such a pretty shade of blue. They made him think of tropical waters in the Caribbean. Could she see the hurt and pain inside of him? He didn't think so, but he felt a sudden urge to share his thoughts. That idea scared him right down to his toes. He quickly released her and took a step back again, but he didn't break the eye contact. Suddenly, his cell phone rang, and he took another step back and looked away, thankful for the distraction.

"Riley," he said brusquely.

"Jake," Dominic answered. "We've got a serious situation. We need you immediately."

Jake listened to the details, all the while securing the weapon Mackenzie had been holding. He then motioned for her to follow him to his car, which was parked in front of his house. Finally, he hung up. "We've got a lead on one of the fugitives we've been chasing, and local police think they have him cornered in a warehouse. We need to move quickly to get to the scene. It might even tie into the Beckett case."

Jake quickly opened the trunk so Mackenzie could verify that her camera and tripod, as well as the bulletproof vest she had been issued, were there. Then the two of them jumped in the front seat of the sedan and headed out. Another vehicle with the other deputies followed closely behind them. The trip across town took around thirty minutes, and when they arrived in the warehouse district, they were met by one of the local police captains. The man was clearly in charge and was communicating by radio with the other officers, who were staked out around the building. Jake focused on the job at hand and paid little attention to Mackenzie, even as she followed him around, pulled out her camera and started filming.

"Okay, Captain, tell me what you've got," Jake said in a matter-of-fact tone once he had introduced himself and the other deputy marshals.

"We got a tip that someone is storing stolen goods in that building," the captain said as Dominic handed Jake a bulletproof vest. "We've seen three men go in, including a man named Bryson Taylor, and so far, nobody has come out. No telling how many were in there to start with, though. Once we pegged his identity, we saw that he was on your most-wanted list and gave you a call."

"Who's Bryson Taylor?" Mackenzie asked, pointing the camera in the captain's direction. The man raised an eyebrow and gave Jake a look, to which Jake shrugged.

"A thief. A pretty good one, actually, although he did finally get captured in Atlanta," Jake answered her. "We've had an outstanding warrant for him for about six months now. He's actually a known associate of Beckett's. That's why I said there's a possibility that these cases are related." He turned his back on the camera and focused again on the captain. "Who owns this building?"

"A holding company named Lincoln Corp. It's rented to a man named Josh Simmons. So far, we haven't found a connection between Simmons and Taylor, but we're checking."

"Did you get an ID for the gents that went in with Taylor?"

The captain shook his head. "We couldn't tell if they were carrying, either. This arrest could go without a hitch or it could get ugly really fast."

Jake tensed his jaw. "Did you get a warrant to search the place?"

"We just got it," Dominic answered. "We called the judge on the way over here. We're good to go in whenever you're ready."

"Good." He turned to Mackenzie, his eyes intense. "Stay put. Do you understand?"

Mackenzie bristled, and Jake could see her spine stiffen. "But…"

"This is not up for debate." He glanced around. "I want you over there, out of the way." He pointed to an area that was well away from the entrance to the building. He wasn't sure if she could get any good shots from that far away, but he really didn't care. He wanted her well out of range if this operation went south. "Stay there. Got it?"

She glared at him but could apparently tell by his expression and posture that he wasn't going to bend.

Finally, she put up her hand in mock surrender. "Fine. But after you've gotten them in custody, I want to record you taking them out of the building. Deal?"

Jake considered her words and then nodded. "Deal. I'll call you on your cell." He looked over to Dominic. "Let's move."

Dominic nodded and relayed the news to the other deputy marshals at the scene, and then the two men started toward the building.

Jake followed Dominic to the warehouse door, his weapon drawn and ready. Dominic radioed their position to the other team members and local law enforcement, while Jake examined the security pad that was by the door. It was an older model and linked to a system that he had dealt with several times in the past. He easily disarmed it and entered the building with Dominic. A rush of cool air met them, but it was dark except for a row of security lights that gave off a soft glow from the high ceiling. The room was filled with pallets and metal shelving filled with boxes and crates of various sizes. In most places, they were stacked almost to the ceiling. Jake felt like a mouse going through a maze as they turned several corners, moving cautiously, guns pointed, all senses on high alert. They heard voices, and Dominic signaled that he was stopping to assess the situation.

"I got too much inventory comin' and goin'. He's

got to clear some of this stuff out of here to make room for the new," said a male voice.

Another man laughed. "Are you gonna tell him that? I'm sure not."

"Somebody has to say it. I'm getting heat from all sides."

Another voice said something that was unintelligible, but Jake could tell that there were at least three different people up ahead. He signaled to Dominic, who gestured back that he was ready for the confrontation.

"Freeze! US Marshals!" Jake and Dominic rounded the stack of boxes, completely taking the men by surprise. Two of the men immediately put their hands up, but the third slowly reached behind his back. His dark eyes darted back and forth between the lawmen as if daring them to stop him.

"The deputy said freeze," said another voice, and Whitney stepped out of the shadows from the other direction, startling the big man whose hand had been moving. Upon seeing yet another 9 mm pointed at this chest, the goon finally shrugged and put his hands up, as well.

"Wise move," Jake said, a hint of irony in his voice. He stepped up behind the hesitant man and cuffed one hand, then another, simultaneously taking the man's gun, which had been hiding in his waistband. Dominic and Whitney cuffed the other two, but Jake raised an eyebrow as he looked closely at the three men.

"Where is Bryson Taylor?"

"Who?" the big man said with a grunt.

Jake pushed the man up against the wall, getting another grunt for his efforts. "I said I want to know where Bryson Taylor is. We saw him come in this building."

"Man, I don't know who you're talkin' about."

Jake knew the thug was lying, especially because the man wouldn't even meet his eyes. He might be able to get some information out of him back at the jail, but for now it wasn't worth wasting his time. Jake grabbed the guy by the shoulder and pushed him toward the other two. "Whitney, I'm going to get these guys out of here. We've got the perimeter covered. You and Dominic start the search for Taylor and clear the building, okay?"

NINE

Mackenzie fiddled with the focus button on her camera as she watched two of the deputy marshals communicate on their radios. She had stayed where Jake had asked her to—near the parked cars and well away from the action—but she still wasn't convinced she would be allowed to get any decent footage of the arrest. A wave of frustration swept over her. Had Jake purposefully put her to the side where she couldn't get any good shots or was he at least going to let her do her job once they made the arrest? She adjusted her bulletproof vest and stretched out a kink in her neck. The vest was so heavy she was surprised they could actually do their job effectively when they were wearing it. To her, it just seemed to get in the way. She glanced again at the large yellow words emblazoned across the vest: US MARSHAL. Yeah, she wore the uniform, but it sure didn't make her feel like part of the team.

Since she had time to spare, she figured now was as good a time as any to text her parents and let them know she was okay. She sent the message and a couple of other work-related texts, thankful that Jake had at least given her a way to continue doing her job. Her phone was her livelihood, and she used it constantly to keep in touch with her customers. Unreturned calls meant lost income. Suddenly her cell phone buzzed with a call. She answered, keeping her eyes on the warehouse door in case Jake emerged with a captive. There was no way she was going to miss out on filming an arrest this time around. Her father's voice rang out, filled with enthusiasm, but she kept watch on the law enforcement officers, ready to hit the record button as soon as the need arose.

"Hey, Dad. I'm a bit busy right now. Can I call you later?"

"Hello, Mackenzie. This will only take a minute. I'm so glad you sent the text with your new number. I just wanted to let you know I ran into Miller again. He said he could fit you in next Thursday for an interview. Does that sound like it will work for you?"

His words surprised her and forced her to take her focus off her surroundings so she could zero in on the call. "Ah, no, Dad. I already have a job. I'm not interested in applying somewhere else. I thought we already talked about this."

She could instantly hear the disappointment filter into her father's tone. "I thought that fire you mentioned might have changed your mind now that you've had some time to think about it. This way you'll get a great starting salary and won't have to begin from scratch again with your business. You could still make movies on the side as time allows."

Mackenzie instantly decided not to tell her parents about the threats to her life. She'd never hear the end of it if they knew she had been shot at on two separate occasions over the last few days and was in protective custody with a group of deputy marshals.

She sighed. Would explaining her feelings about her career choices for the hundredth time really change her father's mind or was it a wasted breath? She decided to take a more forceful approach, hoping she could convince him and quickly get him off the phone at the same time. She needed to be watching the warehouse, not discussing her future via cell phone. "Look, I'm strong. I'm smart. I've got a good business plan, and I can run my production company the way I want to. I'm successful, and I'm doing it on my own without any help from anyone else. Those are all good reasons to stay right where I am, doing what I love."

"I hear you, Mackenzie, but you could have something more stable that offers security and a retirement program if you take this interview. I'm sure Miller's job pays a lot better than what you're making now."

"That is probably the case, Dad, but getting rich was never one of my goals."

A moment passed, then another. "So, you're sure then?" he asked, resignation heavy in his voice.

"Yes. Please tell Miller I won't be able to see him on Thursday."

The cold barrel of the gun pressed against her temple sent a wave of shock down her spine. She froze instantly as the fear coursed through her.

"Don't move, princess." The voice was cold and hard as the man behind her whispered in her ear.

She had been so wrapped up in her conversation that she hadn't even heard him approach. With his empty hand, the man grabbed her phone, turned it off and put it in the back pocket of his jeans.

"Okay, here's the plan." He pushed the gun against her skin even harder. "You're going to come with me to that green sedan to your right. See it?" He waited for her eyes to follow his motion and then continued. "You're not gonna give me any trouble. In fact, you're not gonna scream or make any kind of scene. If anyone takes a look in this direction, you're not gonna signal to them or look distressed. Got it? If you say a single word or freak out in any way, I'm going to pull the trigger. Do you hear me?"

She nodded as another surge of fear swept over her from head to toe. The man pulled her into a crouching position behind the cars so that she was barely visible, and then he pushed her forward toward the green sedan. His touch was rough and forceful and made her even more afraid. He obviously didn't care if he hurt her. They made their way slowly between the cars, leaving Mackenzie's camera still sitting on the tripod and the rest of her equipment stored in the bag on the ground. For a moment, she was scared that her camera would get stolen, but the thought was quickly replaced with a rush of fear for her life. Her camera was replaceable. Right now, her primary concern was just surviving this latest threat.

The man's grip tightened, and the terror shot up her arm. Would anybody even realize she was missing? If so, how long would it take? Jake was wrapped up in his arrest, and she had no idea when or if he would think to include her in his activities. Where was this man taking her? Would she live to see tomorrow? Her contemplations made her stomach turn, and she fought to keep the nausea at bay. She wanted to scream for help, but the man's words and the gun in his hand kept her silent. She didn't doubt his threats and didn't want the last thing she saw in this life to be the white lines painted on the asphalt in the parking lot.

"Get in, princess," the man ordered. He opened the door and motioned to the front passenger seat. She followed his directions, her entire body trembling. Once she was seated, he quickly got behind the wheel and started the engine. The next thing she knew, they were driving out of the parking lot. She wondered fleetingly if she could somehow open the door and jump out of the moving car, but the man kept his pistol pointed in her direction. She was afraid to try it. Would it be worse to die from a bullet wound or from the injuries she would sustain from falling out of a moving car? She hung on to the hope that the man would free her when he was far enough from the warehouse to ensure his escape.

Jake scanned the parking lot, keeping his eyes open for anything unusual as he led the men toward the car. They were all handcuffed, but with Taylor still at large, he didn't want to let down his guard. Normally, he would have preferred to search the building with Dominic and Whitney instead of securing the prisoners, but since he had promised Mackenzie an opportunity to video the arrest, he felt obligated to be the one to take the heat once she realized that she'd missed the action. He hoped that filming him taking the prisoners out of the warehouse would be enough to make her happy. She hadn't answered her phone when he'd called, and he wondered fleetingly just how angry she was going to be when he emerged and she missed the shot completely. She just had to realize that law enforcement work didn't follow a schedule that could be stopped and changed just to accommodate a videographer.

Once outside the building, he noticed her camera was still standing on the tripod where he had told her to go, but there was no sign of Mackenzie. That was odd. He knew the camera was very expensive, and she wouldn't leave it alone for more than a few seconds. If she had decided to leave the area, he was sure she would have taken the camera off the tripod and taken it with her. A frisson of uneasiness swept up his spine. Something was wrong. Very wrong. He pushed the communication link on his radio.

"Dominic, Mackenzie isn't out here in the parking lot where I left her. Did she come in the building?"

"Negative, Jake. I haven't seen her."

"Chris, any sign of Mackenzie?"

"Negative, Jake. I'm just coming around the north end of the building. There's no sign of her."

Just then Jake noticed the green sedan driving slowly away from him. He could see two occupants, and one seemed to have long brown hair, but he couldn't get a good look. "Chris, I've got a green sedan coming your direction. Can you ID either the driver or the passenger?"

While he waited to hear back from Chris, Jake secured the prisoners in the back seat of Dominic's service vehicle by locking their handcuffs to metal rings in the back of the cruiser. A moment later his radio crackled. "Jake, we have a problem. Taylor is driving, and Mackenzie is the passenger. He's waving a gun around. I think she's in trouble."

Jake felt a surge of adrenaline at Chris's words and started running toward his car. "I'm going after them. The prisoners are locked down in Dominic's car. Come cover them and get Whitney and Dominic to follow me."

"Affirmative," Chris answered.

Jake slammed his car into gear and then gunned the engine and spun his tires as he peeled after the last place he had seen the green sedan. He caught a glimpse of it ahead and sped up. He couldn't believe that Mackenzie had been taken hostage. It was entirely his fault that she was in danger. He should never have allowed her to accompany him to the warehouse. There were people out there trying to kill her, and he had let her come to a crime scene to make a movie— and left her unguarded at that. What had he been thinking? He hit the steering wheel as frustration overtook him.

Taylor must have noticed the tail because Jake suddenly saw the sedan swerve around another car and speed up. Jake followed but was only able to get within fifty feet of his quarry before Taylor's car made a hard right onto another street, narrowly missing a large black SUV. Jake tapped the brakes and then hit them harder as he skidded around the corner.

His body hit the driver's-side door hard, despite the seat belt, but he quickly adjusted and jammed the gas again, this time being able to pull up closely behind the green sedan. There was no one in the left lane, so he drew up next to the car and then veered hard to the right, trying to force Taylor off the road. The fenders of the two vehicles crunched as metal scraped against metal, but he slowed down as Taylor pointed his gun at him and took a shot. The bullet shattered the passenger's-side window and showered bits of glass all over Jake, but he sped up and once again pushed his car against the green sedan. Taylor's next bullet went wild. As he pulled up close, Jake caught a glimpse of Mackenzie, whose face was filled with fear. She had her hands over her ears and was scrunched against the car door. Suddenly Jake saw Taylor level the pistol and point it directly at his head.

He hit the brakes and let the green car speed ahead to throw off Taylor's aim, but it didn't stop the onslaught. Taylor merely adjusted and started shooting behind him. Another shot rang out, but it also went wild. Jake ducked low enough to make a smaller target but kept high enough to see to drive. The sedan pulled away and turned down another road to the left, which led away from the city and toward the western side of town and the Lake Talquin area. Jake pulled up beside the green car once again, and another shot ran out. He jerked the wheel to the left, swerving to throw off the man's aim once more. He backed off a bit and pushed the com link on his radio. He called in an update of the situation and his location. Hopefully, some backup would arrive soon, and he could stop being a moving target. He pulled close enough to hit the bumper of the green car and tried once again to push it off the road, but he was hesitant to push too hard because he didn't want to force the car to crash. He wanted Taylor to stop the car, but he didn't want Mackenzie hurt or killed in the process. He hit the bumper again but backed off when he saw Taylor turn and raise the pistol over the back seat. The shot both shattered Taylor's rear window and hit the top right corner of Jake's windshield. A spider crack instantly spread across the glass.

Jake hit the brakes and followed Taylor around another curve. Then he was forced to drop back about forty feet due to an oncoming pickup truck. Taylor swerved quickly around a red coupé, and a minivan forced Jake even farther back. Jake hit the steering wheel in frustration. He couldn't lose her! Mackenzie wasn't going to get hurt or killed on his watch. It just wasn't going to happen. He hit the gas again and was just in time to see Taylor turn to the left on a cross street. Thankfully, there wasn't much traffic on this road, and they had reached the outskirts of town where there were acres of planted pines and little else but a handful of houses and mobile homes. Jake made the turn and his tires squealed, but he dared not slow down too much. Taylor had floored it on the open road and was pulling away from him. Suddenly, a light blue car exited one of the side streets and pulled in front of Jake, and he was forced to slam on his brakes. His tires squealed and spun as he veered around the car. He almost lost control of his vehicle as it fishtailed and swung him in the opposite direction, but he landed on the shoulder of the road.

By the time he had regained complete control of his car and was able to continue the pursuit, the green sedan had disappeared. Jake slowed and studied his surroundings. He saw no other cars on the road, and the only movement was a stray dog crossing the road a hundred feet or so away from him. Many of the streets that led off the main road were unpaved, with a dirt surface, however, and he started looking for plumes of dust or any other signs that would reveal his quarry. He called in an all-points bulletin for the vehicle and gave the dispatcher the tag number as he drove slowly down the road.

After about two miles, he got his first hint of the green sedan's whereabouts. A dirt road leading to the left looked as if someone had recently driven over it, as the dust was just beginning to settle. He did a fast parking job, and pulling out a set of binoculars, scanned a small brick house and carport that were about seventy yards away from the road. There was no car in the carport, but off to the right of the house, he could just make out the shape of a Ford sedan and a hint of green that wasn't quite camouflaged by the brush and trees. He also noticed more dust filling the air above the dirt driveway. Someone had driven over the driveway in the past few minutes, and it was definitely possible that the car parked in the woods was the green sedan he had been following. It wasn't much, but it was the only lead he had at the moment. He glanced at the rusted mailbox, but there was no name—just some faded stickers proclaiming the address. He turned and drove about thirty feet or so out of view of the house and parked again but left his engine running. He pulled out a county map from his glove compartment. The rest of his team would be here soon and then they could start a sweep of the area. He reached for his radio com link button so he could update the rest of his team about his current location but was stopped by the sudden sound of someone tapping on his window. He looked behind him and found himself face-to-face with the barrel of a .357 revolver pointing straight at him.

His eyes followed the gun and were met by Taylor's cold, hard stare.

"I wouldn't touch that radio if I were you, Officer."

Even with the driver's-side window up, it wasn't hard to hear the threat in Taylor's voice. Jake raised his hands and watched as Taylor moved up even closer and opened the driver's-side door of his vehicle. "Turn off the engine and then get out of that car, you hear me?"

Jake nodded, reached for the ignition and cut the engine. He kept his movements slow and easy as he got out of the car. He looked around for any signs of Mackenzie but didn't see anything. Still, she had to be nearby since he had been chasing the sedan and Taylor only minutes before.

"Look, I just want the woman back."

"Shut up," Taylor growled. "Now turn around and put your hands on the hood."

Jake complied and felt Taylor take his weapon from his holster. As Taylor bent to check him for other weapons, Jake suddenly turned and lunged at the man, grabbing for his wrist. The criminal had put Jake's gun in his belt but still had his .357 in his hand. Jake tried to wrench it away from him, and they wrestled for supremacy. Suddenly the gun went flying, and Taylor caught Jake hard in the mouth, cutting his lip against his teeth. Jake answered with a fist to Taylor's gut, and the man staggered back a step and went for the other gun. A swift kick from Jake sent that gun flying, as well. Jake advanced, but Taylor recovered quickly and dove at him, grabbing him against the waist and pushing him hard against the truck. The move knocked the breath out of Jake, but a knee to Taylor's stomach made the man loosen his grip. A second hit made him release Jake and take a step back. The two men stood there, poised and ready to strike, each glaring at the other, waiting for the next attack. They circled each other, keeping a wary distance.

"Where's the woman?" Jake asked as he wiped the blood from his chin.

"She must mean something to you." Taylor laughed. "I'll let you watch when I slit her throat."

Jake shook his head. "If you hurt her, you'll have the entire federal government in your front yard in no time." He narrowed his eyes. "She's going back with me. That's the only way this is going to end. If you try to hurt her, I promise you'll be the one bleedin' out in the dirt." He struck out at the bigger man and connected with Taylor's jaw. Taylor staggered and again lunged for Jake, this time hitting him with such momentum that the two hit the ground hard with Taylor on top. Jake brought up his leg and kicked Taylor at the same time that he pushed at his opponent with all of his strength. The two men rolled, and a few seconds later, Jake was on top, pelting Taylor with his fists. When it was obvious that Taylor was done and no longer a threat, Jake stopped and pulled back, working his fingers to get the pain from the fighting out of his hands. He took a deep breath and glanced around his surroundings, anxious to find Mackenzie and make sure she was safe. He never heard the other man approaching from behind. The blow came so quickly that he scarcely had time to react before the pain radiated across his head and he felt himself drowning in a sea of blackness.

TEN

"So who is this woman anyway?"

Mackenzie heard a chair scrape across the floor in the adjoining room. Her hands were tied behind her with some sort of braided nylon rope, and they'd gagged her with a dirty black bandanna. But beyond that, she was still relatively unscathed. She stood up from where they had thrown her on the bed in a small, undecorated bedroom and moved closer to the door so she could hear more of their conversation and gather whatever she could about their plans. What was their end game? Were they going to kill her? Her heart beat frantically in her chest as she waited to hear some bit of news.

"How should I know? She's got on a vest that says US MARSHAL. She must be another fed. The warehouse was swarming with cops." The voice was low and menacing, and she recognized it as belonging to the man who had abducted her from the parking lot. So far, she had heard at least three other men talking, too, as well as a woman's high-pitched tones.

"Man, the feds are crawlin' all over the place. The timing couldn't be worse."

"Yeah. This really puts a kink in things. I hope the boss has a plan to take care of the situation before it gets any worse." This man's voice was a cross between a whimper and a grumble, and she dubbed him "Whiny" in her head. Even though she couldn't see him, she could imagine the man's words and tone only irritated her abductor. The man who had kidnapped her seemed like the kind who didn't take kindly to criticism of any kind.

There was a pause and then laughter, raucous and deep. Another man snorted. "I'm sure he does. The boss always has a plan."

"Yeah, but he seems worried lately—like things aren't coming together like they should."

"Well, why'd you grab up this woman?" Whiny said. "Seems like the last thing we needed was the cops breathing down on us. Now they'll be out searching for sure."

"She was my insurance policy for my escape. Besides, the boss has a plan to use it for our advantage."

"I think it was dumb to take her."

She heard a slap and a loud thump as if someone had fallen out of their chair. "You're the idiot! You never think beyond the moment." There was another scrape. "Look, the boss needs some time to finish moving the merchandise without interference. If the cops are focused on finding this lady, they won't have time to be chasing the boss. We're the diversion now. Get it?"

Whiny grunted. "Okay, I get it, but I better get paid well for this extra risk I'm taking here. I'm gonna need lots of cash so I can disappear once this is over."

"Don't worry. There's enough to go around, and you'll get what's coming to you. I promise."

Mackenzie cringed at those last words and pulled against the ties on her hands, but the rope only seemed to tighten as she struggled. Her skin burned. *You'll get what's coming to you.* She doubted the whiny man noticed the phrasing, but to her, the words foreshadowed pain and even death, not a large payoff.

She heard footsteps coming in her direction, and she quickly moved back over to the bed. Her abductor opened the door and grinned. "Okay, princess. It's time to take a little ride." He grabbed her arm roughly and pulled her to her feet. He smelled of sweat and old socks, and her nose wrinkled involuntarily. Her fear amplified her senses, and she hoped her aversion didn't show on her face. The last thing she wanted to do was irritate this man any further. He pulled her out the bedroom door and through the kitchen, but she barely had time to glance at the other people before she was outside, standing by the green sedan again. She noticed that the woman she had heard while in the room had reddish-brown hair and one of the men had a brown mustache, but that was about it. The man who'd abducted her opened the back door and pushed her inside. Then he shoved her again when she tried to sit up. "Stay down, do you hear me? Don't make me tell you again. You won't like the results. Got it?"

He laughed and encircled her ankle with one large hand, pulling it close to his hip. "You really think you can get away from me? Think again." This time when she tried to pull away, he held fast to her leg and rubbed his fingers roughly over her skin. "You're pretty. I bet men fawn over you all day long."

The gag kept her from responding, but she shook her head, still pulling against his grip. He laughed again and finally pushed her foot away. He then slammed the car door, leaving her inside. She was no match for his strength, and they both knew it. She shrank back as far as she could against the vinyl bench seat, but there was really no place for her to go. A knot of terror and trepidation pulled and twisted in her stomach. Would she survive the day? What horrors awaited her?

She was left alone with her fears for a good twenty minutes. Then she heard the trunk open. Something heavy was thrown inside, and the entire car shook when the trunk door slammed shut. Suddenly, her abductor and another man jumped in the front seat and the engine roared to life. The car started moving with a groan, and Mackenzie pulled herself to a sitting position and saw a plume of dust swell up behind them as they drove away from the brick house.

"Did you hear that Beckett got arrested?" It was the whiny man again. She could hear the irritation in her abductor's voice when he answered.

"Of course I heard. The boss keeps me informed of what's going on."

"Well, what if Beckett tells them about our plans? What then?"

"You worry too much. Just shut up and leave the thinkin' to me. Everything is going down the way we planned."

"You planned for Beckett to get arrested?"

Mackenzie saw her captor smack the other man. "Of course, not, you fool. But Beckett knows the score. He won't talk to the police. None of our plans have changed. We got most of the merchandise out of the warehouse before the feds arrived, anyway, and they don't even know about the other warehouse. We'll be sitting pretty on the beach with a drink in our hand, living the good life in no time. The boss always makes sure he has a contingency plan. Now stop worrying and keep your mouth shut so I can drive."

Her abductor's voice was gruff and unfeeling, which caused the knot in Mackenzie's stomach to grow and fester. The car went over another bump, and her awkward position made her head knock against the car door. Would they ever let her free?

They drove in silence for about an hour or so, and Mackenzie felt like they were driving pretty fast. Maybe they were on a highway? Then she felt the engine slow as they pulled off and made a series of turns before finally starting down a bumpy dirt road filled with potholes. Her position made it hard for her to keep her bearings, but she tried to take mental notes of anything she could about her captors and the trip in case she was ever able to escape. Another bump knocked her head into the door again, and she quit worrying about the rope around her hands and tried to focus on just keeping herself far enough away from the armrest to keep from getting hurt even further.

She bit into the gag they had forced into her mouth and swallowed hard as a nervous tingle went up her spine. Was the fact that she wasn't blindfolded a problem? Did that mean her abductors didn't care if she saw their faces because they were planning to kill her anyway? So far, she was relatively unscathed apart from a little rough manhandling, but she was terrified that her life would be snuffed out by the criminals surrounding her and she wouldn't live to see another sunset.

Suddenly, the car stopped. She heard her abductor put the car in Park and turn off the engine. Her heartbeat sped up until it felt like it would pop right out of her chest. What would happen to her now?

"Here we go, princess."

She was dragged unceremoniously out of the back seat, and a new wave of fear swept over her. They seemed to be in a very isolated location, and the only thing she saw was a small shack that leaned slightly to the left in front of her. It was surrounded by pine trees and scrub brush. Cicadas chirped in the distance, and a swarm of mosquitoes seemed to buzz near her ears as soon as she left the vehicle. The heat was oppressive despite the cover the trees provided, and she felt sweat start to gather on her neck, although she wasn't altogether sure if it was the hot July sun or the cold eyes of her abductor that made the moisture form on her skin. She couldn't hear any other cars or noises that signaled civilization was nearby, and from the sounds of insects and birds, she imagined they were deep in the woods in a rural area either still in the Florida panhandle or on the southern edge of Georgia. She was alone. Correction. She was alone with two ruffians. Were they going to kill her? She stumbled as nausea turned her stomach, and her abductor grabbed her arm as the whiny man leered nearby.

"This way, darlin'."

She flinched at his touch, and the man laughed and stroked her hair suggestively.

Mackenzie jerked away from his touch and ended up losing her balance and falling to the ground. Her hands were still tied behind her, and she groaned as pain radiated up her arms. She scooted away from her abductor and kicked a cloud of sand at him, but he only laughed at her attempts to keep him away. He bent and grabbed her ankle to stop her escape and then reached over and secured her arms with cold, unfeeling hands. His body odor overwhelmed her and his stale breath polluted her face. Her gag still kept her from speaking, but she wailed loudly as the fear made her frantic to escape. She struggled against his grip and felt sand and bits of rock and debris embed into her skin beneath her clothing.

Her abductor leaned closer to adjust his grip, and she brought up her knee hard, hitting him in the ribs. She instantly realized her actions were a mistake. A fire lit in his eyes, and he drew his hand back and slapped her hard, jarring her teeth and jaw. "Where do you think you're goin', huh? There's no escaping me. Now, quit fighting." She slowed her motions but couldn't stop her arms from trembling from exertion. He turned his head and spoke to Whiny. "What are you doin' just standing there? Help me get her up."

Whiny jumped to do the other man's bidding, and the two unceremoniously pulled Mackenzie to her feet. The smaller man must have felt pity for her, and he leaned close to her ear.

"Easy there. Nobody's going to hurt you anymore

as long as you do what he says. We just need you out of the way for a few days." His words calmed Mackenzie a bit, but the fear was still there in the pit of her stomach. Was he lying just to get her cooperation? Even if he was, there wasn't much she could do to defend herself or escape. She also doubted he would really oppose the bigger man and come to her defense if he really wanted to hurt her.

She let them pull her toward the shack, her mind spinning. She'd have to wait and watch for a better opportunity to escape. Somehow, she was going to get out of here alive. She didn't know how, but she was going to give it everything she had. She thought back to the words she had spoken to her father only hours before. *I'm strong. I'm smart...* Her entire life she had been self-assured and confident that she could do anything on her strength alone. Maybe it was time to rethink that strategy. Maybe she needed a bit of help despite her claims to the contrary.

Dear God, please help me. God would never leave her or forsake her. She had to remember that. She said another quick prayer for help and instantly felt a sense of peace start to soothe her frazzled nerves. She quietly acknowledged that she wouldn't be able to escape this situation without His help. She needed God in her life now more than ever.

The building was musty and hot and smelled slightly of rot and decay. It appeared to be a one-room hunting shack of sorts, with a cot on one side, a couple of shelving units and a small dresser in one of the corners. On one side of the room there was a kitchen sink, a stove and a few wooden cabinets, and in the middle of the room sat a rustic table and chairs with a layer of dust and bug carcasses. There was one small window over the sink and another on one of the walls, both with faded red gingham curtains around the edges. A single door was on the back wall, and she imagined it led to a bathroom.

She heard the door shut behind them with a snap, and she jumped at the sound. Now what was going to happen? She turned slightly and was met by her abductor's smiling face. He took a step closer and then another until he was only a few short inches from her face. He was so close that she could see the gray flecks in his dark eyes and the ruddy flush of his skin. "Yep, you sure are a pretty one."

She took a step back and then another, shaking her head as she did so. She bumped against the table, and the man moved closer and grabbed her hair, letting it shift between his fingers. She pulled her head back, but instead of releasing her, he grabbed her hair in a fist and pulled her roughly toward him. She groaned at the awkward angle of her neck and grimaced from pain. He pulled her forward a few more steps and then forced her to sit in one of the dirty chairs.

"Tie her up good and strong," he said roughly to Whiny. "We don't want her getting away." She felt rope across her chest as the smaller man complied, but her eyes never left her abductor. He slowly released her hair, and she pulled her head away from him in the only act of defiance left to her.

Whiny stood, his job complete. Her abductor bent to examine the other man's work and then stepped away, apparently satisfied. He motioned toward the door. "Let's go get the other one," he said heavily.

Mackenzie's heart raced. They had abducted someone else, as well? A new anxiety swelled within her. Who was the other person? Was it a man or a woman? Was he a criminal and another threat, or someone who could ultimately help her escape? Various scenarios played out in her mind, but none of them were good. Tears formed in her eyes, but she blinked them away as best she could. This wasn't the time to fall apart. She needed to stay alert and think. She closed her eyes and said another silent prayer. She definitely needed God and His help to endure.

The front door opened again, and the two men entered, pulling a body with them. From the angle of the chair, she could tell it was a man, but not much else. She jerked involuntarily as they let him fall to the floor with a thud, several feet behind her. Whoever it was must have been out cold or dead because she heard no sounds of struggle as they kicked him with their boots.

"Man, he was heavy."

"No kidding." There was a pause. "Good grief! I got his blood on my shirt." She cringed at the words and heard the two men rustling around in the room and cabinet doors opening and closing. Then her abductor stood back in her line of sight, holding a small kitchen towel and wiping the blood from his hands. He grinned at her, almost appearing to feed off her fear.

"Don't worry, princess. I'll come back for you

soon. We don't want you dead. We just want you out of the way for a few days."

He touched her shoulder and squeezed it roughly. She flinched, but since she was tied to the chair there wasn't anywhere for her to go. He leaned closer and drew a finger slowly down her cheek. She pulled her head away as far as she could but still couldn't avoid his touch. He laughed, throwing the towel near the sink, and then punched Whiny in the arm. "All right. Let's get out of here." She heard their steps as they left the room. The door slammed behind them, and she heard a lock engage. A few minutes later, the car engine roared to life once again, and the vehicle drove slowly away from the shack.

Mackenzie breathed a sigh of relief but then immediately focused on her surroundings. If the men were coming back, she had to figure out a way to escape. Now. She didn't know if they'd be back in an hour or if they would leave her like this for days, but either way, she didn't plan on being here when they returned. She listened carefully and could just make out the sounds of the other person's breathing. Good. Whoever it was wasn't dead, but he obviously wasn't in good shape, either. Maybe she could help him, and they could work together to form an escape plan. Before she could do that, though, she needed to get out of the bindings.

ELEVEN

Mackenzie's mind whirled. The first thing she needed to do was get out of this chair, or at least turn it around so she could see what else was in the room with her. She tried to get rid of the gag, but no matter how she struggled, she couldn't loosen the filthy material. She paused for a moment, thinking, and then started rocking the chair. She wasn't sure making the chair fall to the floor was really her best option since she didn't know what was down there, but she hoped that somehow, she could get the ropes and gag off if she could rub them or catch them against something sharp on the floor. It was the only thing to do. The chair hit the ground with a bang, and more pain radiated up her arms. She gasped and paused to regroup for a moment, waiting for the ache to subside.

It was then that she heard it. A small groan escaped from the other person in the room, and then she heard movement as if he was struggling to sit up. Her first thought was that the stranger could help her, but what if he was another criminal that had crossed the men who had abducted her? Maybe the other person was just as bad as or worse than the men who had left them here… She really hadn't gotten a good look at him when her abductor and the whiny man had brought him into the cabin. In fact, she'd barely seen more than a motionless dark shape. Fresh fear swept from her head to her toes, and she put all the effort she could into inching herself along the floor, feeling for anything that could help her get herself free from her bindings. The floor seemed to be made of wood, and it was old and rough against her skin. She hoped there was something on the floor, perhaps a doorstop or something similar, which would help her at least take off the gag so she could breathe normally. She pushed again, rubbing her hands against the rough wooden planks and ignoring the pain from her arms as a sliver of desperation swept over her. Wasn't there any way she could free herself? She pushed again and winced as a nail from a floorboard caught her face and tore into her skin. She grimaced but felt the first seeds of hope start to sprout. She maneuvered against the nail, pulling and pushing until she finally freed herself of the gag.

She worked her jaw a bit, and the new angle she was in gave her a better look at her surroundings. The floor was filthy, and she could see an assortment of spiderwebs and bug carcasses in every direction. Since those were currently the least of her problems, though, she tried to focus instead on getting her hands untied. She maneuvered her arms and pulled the rope against the nail. It only seemed to make the knots tighter. The other person groaned again, and she worked more frantically at the rope, but to no avail. No matter what she did, the knots just seemed to tighten and cause the rope to bite deeper into her wrists.

"Mackenzie?"

The voice was soft but recognizable. "Jake?" She quickly pushed against the floor and tried to move the chair so she could see him, but the chair caught against the table leg and got wedged so tightly that it was hard to move. Even though she couldn't see him, her heart soared. With Jake nearby, she knew her odds of survival had just increased exponentially.

"Are you okay?" he said roughly.

"Yeah, but they tied me to this chair. Now I'm stuck." She yanked again, and the wood creaked with her efforts but didn't give.

"Whoa, hold on there…ah…give me a sec, and I'll help you."

She heard him shuffling behind her and then felt his hands working on the ropes. A few minutes later, the binding fell away. She was finally able to stretch out her arms, take the rest of the ropes off and pull herself up to sitting position. Her muscles nearly sang with relief.

"Thanks!" She turned to him. "Are you okay?" Her words of gratitude were quickly forgotten as she reached for his head and touched his cheek gently. Blood had caked on the left side of his head and surrounded a nasty-looking wound. Head wounds always bled a ridiculous amount, and this one was no exception. The blood had dripped down his ear and neck and left a dark stain on his shirt.

He grimaced and sat back, moving slowly. "I've got a bit of a headache."

"I don't doubt it!" she exclaimed, and then lowered her voice once she realized that loud volumes would only worsen his pain. She moved closer and gingerly examined his wound. "You're going to need stitches."

"We'll see if I get to a hospital in time. If I don't, I'll just have a really cool new hairstyle."

Mackenzie laughed. "I can't believe you're joking at a time like this." She stood and glanced around the room. Then she moved to the sink and tried the faucet. Brown water spurted out as air bubbles cleared the line, but after a few minutes the water ran clear. She left the water running for a few minutes as she looked through the cabinets to see if she could find any kitchen towels or other fabric. The bloody hand towel her abductor had used still lay on the floor, but she continued searching, hoping she could find something else. She finally found a somewhat clean dish towel in the last drawer she searched and quickly wet it and returned to Jake's side. He still hadn't stood and instead had scooted back and was leaning against the wall with his eyes closed. Gingerly, she began wiping away the blood.

"Are you hurt anywhere else? Your bottom lip looks swollen."

"It's not that bad. My ribs hurt a bit, but I think the head wound is the worst of it."

She returned to the sink to rinse out the towel and then resumed cleaning the wound. His muscles tightened under her ministrations, but after a few minutes he seemed to relax and his eyes slowly drifted closed again. The gash had stopped bleeding but started again as she worked. Still, there was dirt around the wound, so she felt like the cleaning was necessary and the slight amount of bleeding was actually helping her to get small bits of sand and debris out of the cut. Once the wound was cleaned, she rinsed the towel again and held it against the wound to stop the bleeding. She gently took Jake's hand and placed it on top of the fabric. "Here, hold this on the wound for a sec while I look for some bandages."

He nodded his assent, and she got up and searched the rest of the cabin for a first aid kit. There wasn't a lot to search since the one-room cabin was small and only had a few sticks of furniture, but in the bathroom she found what she was looking for in the bottom of the cabinet under the sink. The first aid kit was small, but it contained a tube of Neosporin and some gauze and medical tape. The date had passed on the tube of antibiotic ointment, but it was still better than nothing. She returned, dressed his wound and then gently touched his lip to assess the damage.

He opened his eyes at her touch, and she gave him a smile as she enjoyed the warmth in those green depths. His presence alone had made her worst fears dissipate, even in his injured state. "I think you're going to make it, Deputy."

He reached for her hand and squeezed it, and surprisingly, didn't let go. "Thanks, Doc."

"You're welcome." She sat and leaned against the wall next to him, enjoying the feeling of his fingers interlocking with hers. His presence and touch were very comforting.

Neither spoke for a few minutes, and Mackenzie said a small prayer of thanks, just letting the peaceful feelings drift over her and replace the anxiety. God had heard her pleas, and He'd sent her help. She didn't know how all of this would end, but at least she wouldn't be alone.

Finally, Jake gave her hand a gentle squeeze. "Mackenzie, I need you to pretend you're a detective, okay? Start with anything you might have seen or heard since you were taken from the parking lot, and don't stop until you get to the part where I just woke up."

Mackenzie raised an eyebrow, thinking back. "I'm not sure what's important and what's not..."

"No worries. Just tell me everything you can remember. I'll ask questions along the way to help you out."

"Okay." She brushed the hair out of her eyes. "I was waiting with my camera when this man forced me at gunpoint to get in the car with him, and then he took me to this house in the country where there were three other men and a woman. I never got a good look at them, but I heard the different voices. The man who abducted me tied my hands, gagged me and then locked me in a bedroom. He talked with the others about what to do next. A little while later, he forced me into the back seat of that green car, and then about half an hour later, he came back and put something heavy in the trunk. I guess it was you."

Jake nodded, apparently absorbing the information. "The man that took you from the parking lot was Bryson Taylor. He was the fugitive we were after at the warehouse, and I recognized him when I was chasing you. He must have slipped through the perimeter and grabbed you as a bargaining chip in case he got captured." Jake's soft Southern voice was comforting, but his words chilled Mackenzie even further.

"That was part of it. I mean, when I was locked in that bedroom, I heard them say something about how kidnapping me was also a diversion, and if the cops were busy looking for me, they wouldn't be paying attention to the boss and the fact that he was moving merchandise, or something like that. I'm not sure I understood them correctly. It's hard to put the pieces together so they all make sense." She took a breath. "I also remember the woman saying they needed to move your car and put it on the other side of town so the police would be looking in the wrong area. I think she was trying to give the other men something to do to keep them from fighting because they were really getting upset with each other."

"Did they ever mention Beckett's name?"

Mackenzie nodded. "Yes. The man with the whiny voice asked if the other knew Beckett had been arrested. He was worried Beckett would talk and implicate him."

Jake sat quietly for a few minutes, absorbing the information. His head felt like it would split right open, and his ribs hurt with each breath he took, but he willed the pain away and tried to concentrate on the facts. "I have a theory. Bryson Taylor is a known thief with a long rap sheet. I'm thinking both he and Beckett are somehow connected to Lager, either directly or indirectly. Either way, I would imagine that my team ended up seizing a boatload of stolen merchandise at the warehouse once the dust cleared. Taylor's team must have some more stolen merchandise stashed at another location, and to be safe, they're going to try to move it, just in case we're able to figure out where it is. There are probably clues in the warehouse about where they're keeping everything, and they know it's just a matter of time before we discover their other hiding place. By taking you and me and keeping us hidden, they're probably hoping the police will be so busy looking for us that they can buy enough time to either sell the stuff or stash it somewhere safe and recoup some of their losses." He sighed. "Taylor is right. You can be sure they are out there looking for us, Mackenzie. They won't stop until they find us."

Jake opened his eyes again and glanced at their hands. He then turned and met her eyes, his feelings of worry suddenly intense. "Are you sure they didn't hurt you? Taylor has a rough reputation. He can be downright mean when he wants to be."

Mackenzie shook her head. "No. I'm okay. Really. I would tell you if they had."

Jake raised an eyebrow. "Would you?" He could see a slight flush in her cheeks, but he couldn't keep the protectiveness out of his voice.

"Yes. I promise. He scared me, but I'm okay. Really."

He leaned back, satisfied, and closed his eyes again. "Okay. What happened next?"

"We drove for about an hour, made a few turns,

and then came up a bumpy road until we ended up here. I guess this is an old hunting shack. I didn't see any other houses nearby when I got out of the car. Wherever they stashed us, I have a feeling we're out in the middle of nowhere."

"Did they say anything about coming back?"

"Yes, but they didn't say when."

"Did you hear them mention any other names?"

Mackenzie shook he head. "Beckett was the only name they mentioned. I can't even really describe the others. One man had a mustache. The woman's hair was kind of a reddish brown. I'm sorry I don't know more. I only got a glimpse of them."

He squeezed her hand again. "You're doing great." He willed his head to stop spinning so he could concentrate. He probably had a concussion from the blow, which would explain the dizziness and nausea he was feeling. What he needed was a few hours of rest so his body could recover from his head injury, but it was blatantly obvious that he wasn't going to get it. If Taylor and his buddy were coming back, it behooved them both to clear out as quickly as they could before they returned. He didn't remember Taylor having any murder charges on his rap sheet, but he wouldn't put it past him. The man was malicious—Jake had seen a coldness in his eyes when they'd fought by his truck, and he didn't want to experience another confrontation where Mackenzie could get caught in the crossfire.

He glanced over at Mackenzie and enjoyed the softness of her hand. He had to admit that she was handling this whole situation amazingly well. Most people he knew would be panic-stricken by now, with abundant tears and hysterics. Mackenzie was one tough cookie. She had gently doctored his wound, and he found her touch strangely comforting. He hadn't felt truly attracted to anyone in a long time, but now, even with the gentlest contact, sparks seemed to be flying between them. Her hair was in disarray and her face was smudged with dirt, but he still found her incredibly beautiful. Her eyes were simply mesmerizing.

He shook himself slightly to clear his head. What happened to his resolve to remain a loner? Thinking about Mackenzie wasn't going to get them back to civilization, either, and she was counting on him to save them. He could see it in her eyes. He needed to think.

Dear God, help me focus. Please take away some of this pain so I can protect Mackenzie and keep her safe. Give me the strength I need to persevere. I know You're with me. Please guide me and help me make good decisions to get us both out of here.

He gritted his teeth, confident that God would see them through. "Is there anything else you remember? Anything at all?"

She looked thoughtful for a minute and then shrugged. "Not really, but there was something I thought was a bit strange. Over the last few days, it seems like someone has been trying to kill me because of my movies, but these guys don't know I'm a videographer, or at least they haven't made the connection, even though Taylor abducted me when I was standing by my camera. They think I'm a fed of some sort because of the vest I'm wearing."

Jake didn't know how that fit into the puzzle, but he stored it away in his mind just in case. "The less they know the better." He felt his pockets. "Okay, they took my phone and my gun. Do you happen to still have your cell phone?"

Mackenzie shook her head. "Nope. Taylor took it at the parking lot, and later he smashed it with his boot."

Jake's eyes wandered around the room, taking in the details. "Tell me about this place. Are we locked in?"

"There's only the one door, and it's locked up tightly from the outside. I think I heard some sort of chain rattling on the door. There are only the two windows you see, but both of them have iron bars covering them—presumably to keep strangers and critters from breaking in. I think we're at some sort of hunting camp, and if we're still west of Tallahassee, I'd imagine that we're near the Ochlocknee River Wildlife Management Area. I think people do deer and hog hunting around here."

"Any food?"

"Nope. There's a small refrigerator, but it's empty, and there's nothing in the cabinets. I doubt that anybody's been out here in a few months. I think it was a blessing that I found the first aid kit."

"I think you're right." He leaned forward and tried to stand but staggered as dizziness swept over him. A moment later he was back on the floor, his head swimming in darkness.

TWELVE

"Jake?" Mackenzie caught the deputy marshal as he fell and eased him back to the floor of the cabin. *Wow, he's heavy*, she said to herself as she maneuvered him back into a sitting position by the wall. What was the proper treatment for a head injury? She racked her brain, trying to remember the basic first aid she had been taught at her CPR class. Surely they had taught something about what to do when someone you worked with had been bashed in the head and you were stuck in the middle of nowhere?

"I'm...okay. I think... I just moved a little too quickly."

His voice surprised her. She thought he had blacked out, but apparently he hadn't checked out completely. "Yeah, and I'm the queen of England."

Jake winced, but it turned into a smile. "Your Majesty..."

"Look, I've been thinking," Mackenzie stated, ignoring his jibe. "You're in no condition to be out walking around, but if we can figure a way out of this building, I can go for help."

"You could get lost," Jake answered quietly.

"I'll admit I'm no Sacagawea, but…"

"What?"

"Sacagawea. You know, the Native American girl who served as a guide to Lewis and Clark when they were exploring the West."

Jake raised an eyebrow. "My head feels like it's leaking out of my ears. I'll have to try to remember my history lessons a little later."

Mackenzie smiled. "All right, Deputy. We'll talk about it after we figure a way out. Why don't you sit tight for a minute." She stood and examined the front door. It was a solid slab of wood with no windows. She pulled against it, but it was obviously locked from the outside. She had to admit that it was a formidable barrier. She moved to the windows and looked carefully at the iron bars that covered the glass. If the house had been built to code, then there would probably be some way to escape the bars to prevent the occupants from dying in a house fire, but by the looks of the shack, she doubted any part of it would actually pass a building inspection. Apparently, the bars were attached from the outside and bolted to the walls to keep predators away, which also meant there was no way to access them from the inside.

She went back to the front door and examined it again, her mind whirling. Maybe she was making this too difficult. She returned to the cabinets and started looking through the drawers.

"Eureka!"

Jake looked up, a question in his eyes. "Did you find a way out?"

"I think so. Give me five more minutes and I'll let you know." She returned to the front door and went to work on the hinges, hitting the pins with the hammer and screwdriver like a chisel until she could work them out with her fingers. She knew the noise was probably making Jake's headache worse, but she did her best to keep it at a minimum. A few moments later, she pulled on the door and it opened—hinge side first. She looked at the lock on the outside of the door and smiled. If she hadn't thought of taking apart the hinges, the lock would have secured the door with no questions asked. It was a heavy-duty combination lock that looked to be commercial grade.

Thank You, God, for showing me the way out. She looked back over at Jake, who had noticed her success and gave her a round of applause and a crooked smile. Despite his support, she could tell by his expression that he was still hurting. Maybe she should add something to that prayer. *God, please help Jake with his injuries, and help us get back to town safely. We really need Your help.*

She returned to Jake's side. "What next?"

"You're a pretty smart girl, aren't you?"

"Sometimes I get things right, like I was thinking that if we're going to be walking, I should look for a canteen so the heat doesn't get us. It's got to be about a hundred degrees out there. Any other ideas?"

"Yeah, look for a flashlight and any type of weapon. I don't know how long it's going to be before we find help, and since Taylor took my gun, I'd like to be armed if we run across them again."

"I don't remember seeing either, but I'll take a look."

"I also wouldn't mind a couple of ibuprofen or aspirin if you happen across one or two." She nodded and headed to the kitchen area.

Jake watched her dig through the drawers and felt an admiration for her building within him. He was suddenly seeing a totally different side of her. He had to admit the child he remembered was gone, and Mackenzie Weaver was all grown up. She was also much more than just pretty packaging on the outside. Despite his general cynicism of people, he had to admit that this lady was worth a second look.

He paused a moment and analyzed that thought. It had been a while since any woman had caught his attention, and even longer since he had actually done anything about those feelings. It was simpler that way—with fewer complications. Simple was good. Simple was easy. And from a romantic standpoint, being alone meant there was no one to let you down or cause any pain. Still, he couldn't deny that Mackenzie had caught his attention and sparks were starting to fly when they were together. When she had touched his lip earlier to check his injury, he'd felt a sudden urge to kiss her that had been almost overwhelming.

He watched her for a few minutes as she searched the cabin and then closed his eyes. It was hard to see her doing all of the work while he was sitting on the floor, but he was really hurting. Whoever had knocked him out had really gone overboard when they'd bashed his head. His brain felt like it was slosh-ing around in his skull every time he moved. Was he going to even be able to walk out of here? Nausea twisted his stomach.

"Okay, I found an old water bottle, and I actu-ally found a flashlight. The batteries were corroded, though, so I don't think it's worth carrying along un-less you've seen the Energizer bunny nearby. Also, no gun, no knife, but—" She pulled out a plastic gro-cery bag filled with some black material. "I did find a mosquito net and a bit of rope. This ought to come in handy if we can't make it back to the real world by nighttime and have to camp outside. Without this, I imagine the mosquitoes will carry us away."

Jake smiled. He was glad she could keep her sense of humor. The day's events must have terrified her. "Good thinking." He tried to stand up and gingerly used the wall to help himself rise. When he looked over at Mackenzie again, her arms were crossed and her right eyebrow was raised.

"Seriously? You're going to try to walk a few miles when you can't even stand up?"

"I can stand…" he growled.

"Sure, if we take the cabin along with us for you to lean against." She moved closer, and he could see the flecks of blue in her clear, pale eyes. "Give me a break. You've got a serious concussion and you need rest. Why don't you sit back down before you fall down?" She looked around the room and then turned back to him. "On second thought, why don't I help you over to that cot? You can lie down and rest for a couple of hours, and I'll walk down the road a little bit to make sure there's not a house right down the road with a telephone inside."

"That's actually a pretty good idea. I changed my mind—you should go without me. Just keep walking until you find help, and then let them know where I am. If you follow the road, you'll eventually find civilization."

Her eyes rounded. "Jake, I'm letting you rest. That's it. I'll go and explore the area, and then come back and check on you. You're hurt worse than I thought, and I'm not leaving you alone out here." Taking his arm, she gently led him over to the cot and then helped lower him down and get situated.

Jake was touched by her sentiment, but he didn't want her in jeopardy any longer than she had to be. "Look, it makes sense. We don't know when those guys are coming back—it could be an hour, it could be days." He caught her eye and held it. "I don't want you here when they do come back. Do you hear me? It's too dangerous. I've seen Taylor's rap sheet. He's not kind to women."

"And maybe they were just full of hot air and they're never coming back." She took his hand and squeezed it. "I'll look at the tire tracks on the road to see which way we came into this place, and then walk that direction. That way I'll see them driving up the road if they're heading back. If I don't find help in an hour, I'll come back and we'll start out together. That should give you an opportunity to rest up for the walk. Hopefully, there's another hunting shack just a mile or so down the road complete with hunters and a cell phone. Deal?"

A part of Jake knew that he should argue for her to get as far away from the cabin as possible. Taylor and his friends could return at any time and he was genuinely worried for her safety. His brain felt fuzzy, however, and it was hard to really focus on how to convince her. What he wouldn't give for some extra strength Excedrin! He looked at her determined expression and gave up trying. He did need the rest and wouldn't be much good to her if he fainted along the road because he did too much too soon. A couple of hours of sleep would definitely help him regain his sense of purpose. "Deal, but please be careful."

Mackenzie stood and walked to the door. Then she turned and looked back at Jake. His eyes were already closed, and it was obvious he was in a great deal of pain. Her stomach growled as she headed out and started making her way down to the road. Breakfast had been a long time ago, and she hoped she could find help soon. What was the likelihood that she could find a friendly face within a mile or so? She looked down at the tire tracks and started east, following them in the dirt. She doubted there was anyone within ten miles or more of where they'd been stashed, but she wasn't one to give up without a fight. As brave as she'd tried to be around Jake, she had to admit that Taylor scared her right down to her toes. The man was evil. She shivered involuntarily, remembering his touch when he'd slid his finger down her cheek.

The air was stuffy with humidity, and sweat instantly coated Mackenzie's skin as she began to walk.

She tried to stay in the shade as much as possible, but there was no escaping the perspiration. Soon her shirt was sticking to her back. She walked for what seemed like a good half hour, but she didn't see any other signs of life besides the mosquitoes that kept buzzing around her ears and a few cardinals. After about fifteen minutes, she came upon a fork in the road. The new branch wasn't traveled much, as evidenced by the overgrown plants that nearly covered the tire marks, but she turned anyway, hoping that the road was really a driveway that led to a house or at least another shack that was better equipped than the one Bryson Taylor had locked them in. She smiled as she turned a bend and came across a small clapboard house. It was old but seemed to be in decent shape. It even had a screened-in porch. She looked around carefully for signs of life and, seeing none, tried the front screen door. It was locked. Disappointment swept over her, but she circled the building, looking for the back door. She found it and pulled against the knob and then jumped back as a skink quickly darted behind a cement block on the ground, the blue tail still partially visible.

Man, they sure move fast, she said to herself. She tried the knob again and breathed a sigh of frustration. Locked. She turned and surveyed the yard surrounding the house. There was a small pole barn that was just big enough to put a boat under to protect it from the weather and a rusted-out old refrigerator whose door hung sadly on bent hinges. She saw nothing that seemed even marginally useful. There was obviously no one home, and she imagined that the

owner was a weekend fisherman or maybe a snow-
bird that only used the house for a few winter months.
Either way, she doubted there was a working phone
inside or that anybody was coming back soon to help
rescue them.

Her stomach rumbled. Maybe no phone was inside, but a granola bar or some other snack would be a
great find, and she sure wouldn't mind finding some
pain medication for Jake. She had a thought and returned to the back door and then moved the cement
block. A smile crossed her lips as she spotted the key.
Her mother had always kept a key under a rock by
the back door, and apparently, it was a tradition that
other folks followed, as well. She opened the door and
entered a small living room. The house wasn't much
bigger than the shack where she had been imprisoned,
but it at least had a separate bedroom.

"Hello? Is anybody here?" She didn't really expect
an answer, and a quick tour of the place proved her
theory correct. Dust covered most of the furniture,
and it was obvious that no one had been in the house
for a few weeks at least. Her heart sank as she realized
that as she had suspected, the one thing she needed
most—a phone—was nowhere in sight. She searched
through the drawers in the bedroom and opened the
closet, but she didn't find anything useful there or
in the bathroom. She moved to the kitchen area and
looked through the cabinets. No granola bars met her
eyes, but she did find three cans of soup and two cans
of tuna. She searched through the drawers and found
a cloth tote bag. She then filled it with the food and a
few other items she found, including a half-full bot-

tle of Tylenol. At least the visit hadn't been a total waste of time.

A wave of guilt swept over her. She couldn't just steal the stuff, even if she was in a desperate situation. She had no money on her, but she did see a notepad and paper in one of the kitchen drawers. She made a quick list of what she had taken and then explained what had happened. She promised to pay for the items if the owners would just call her home or cell number and tell her what she owed them, and she added her phone number on the bottom. There. That should do it. She looked around the room one last time and then headed back to Jake and the fishing shack.

It seemed even hotter on her return trip, and the air was thick and stifling, even when she was sticking to the shade. She made it back to the main road and turned toward the hunting shack where Jake was waiting. Suddenly, a noise behind her made her jump. Was that a car engine coming toward her? Her heart fluttered, and she quickly looked for cover, choosing to dive behind a palmetto bush just as the car approached. Could the car be their salvation? All they needed was a Good Samaritan who was willing to either give them a ride to the hospital or let them borrow a cell phone. Either would do nicely in her book, and beggars couldn't be choosers. Her excitement quickly turned to dread, though, as she recognized the green sedan that Taylor had used when he had abducted her. There only seemed to be two people in the car, but she couldn't quite determine if it was Taylor driving or not. She flattened herself against the ground, praying fervently that the men in the car didn't see her as they passed. Now what was she going to do? The car passed by without stopping, but Mackenzie's heart was still beating frantically as she watched it head toward the fishing shack. She couldn't think of a single way to help Jake, and she imagined that he was probably sleeping and wouldn't even be aware of the men's approach or arrival. She ran after the car, keeping to the woods and out of the driver's sight, trying to come up with a way to help Jake before it was too late. What would the men do when they discovered Mackenzie had escaped? Would they take their anger out on the injured man? Jake was strong and impressively athletic, but with his head wound, the other men surely had the advantage, especially since they outnumbered her lawman. *Her* lawman. She let that thought go without further analysis and tried to focus on the problem at hand. How could she warn Jake that trouble was heading toward him like a hurricane?

THIRTEEN

Jake stirred at the sound of the car engine and was instantly alert as he heard the car doors open and shut. He had been dozing off and on ever since Mackenzie had left, and he had to admit that the rest had done him good. He would still give his right arm for a bottle of pain reliever, but the nausea seemed to have vanished. When he slowly sat up, he discovered that the dizziness had disappeared, as well. He looked quickly around the cabin to see if he could find anything that he could use as a weapon to protect himself. Not finding anything else in the sparsely furnished room, he ended up grabbing the lamp from the end table. He removed the shade and moved silently to the wall by the broken front door. He heard footsteps on the dry pine needles outside as someone approached, and then a voice muttered, "What the…"

The entire shack seemed to rattle as the first visitor kicked in the door and barreled through the door frame.

Jake brought the lamp down hard on the man's head as he entered, and the man crumpled as glass

shards scattered across the floor. Taylor was right behind the fallen man, however, and his eyes widened
in surprise at the sight of Jake wielding the broken
lamp. Jake still had a large piece of the lamp base in
his hand, and he threw it at Taylor as he stepped over
the body and moved back, looking for anything else
that could be used to slow Taylor down. There was an
old metal fishing gear box on the counter, and Jake
grabbed it and threw it, as well. Taylor deflected the
blow and continued his charge. He grabbed Jake in a
football-style tackle and struck him in the chest, and
the two men backed up and hit the wall hard from
the force of the blow. Jake put his fists together and
brought them down forcefully on Taylor's back. Releasing him, the man staggered and then took a step
back. Jake followed with an uppercut to the man's
jaw, but Taylor didn't go down, despite the blood that
was now dripping from his bottom lip. Instead, he
straightened and rolled his shoulders as if loosening
up for a boxing match. He wiped his bloody mouth
against his sleeve and smiled.

"That the best you can do, Officer? I thought those
federal boys taught you how to fight better than that.
You punch like my ten-year-old sister."

Jake ignored the jibe, his stance ready. When Taylor swung at his head, he deflected the blow with his
left arm and hit the fugitive hard with his right. He
felt the man's nose break under the force of the blow.

Taylor staggered and fell back against the floor
when Jake caught him again in the stomach with a
quick one-two punch.

That should keep you down, Jake thought silently,

but to his surprise, Taylor rolled and was on his feet again in a matter of moments, standing near the open doorway to the shack. The blood from his nose was dripping down onto the front of his shirt, but the man barely seemed to notice it.

"Come on, Deputy. Let's go again," Taylor taunted, motioning with his hands.

Jake was tired. The fight had sapped what little strength he had managed to regain, and his head was beginning to pound again. He blinked and gritted his teeth, willing himself to stay standing. At this point, he wasn't so sure he could beat Bryson Taylor, but he had to try. He had to protect Mackenzie. If he couldn't stop him now, one or both of them might just end up on a slab in the morgue. Suddenly Jake heard a loud thunk. Slowly, the light left Taylor's eyes and the man fell forward, first to his knees and then all the way to the ground. Standing behind him was Mackenzie, holding a tote bag that she had just swung at Taylor's head with all her might. She had a fearful yet satisfied look on her face.

Jake stepped forward and checked Taylor, first finding his pulse and then searching for any weapons. The man was alive but out cold, and would have a serious headache when he came to. Jake glanced back up at Mackenzie. "Welcome back." He pulled his own gun, which the man had stolen from him earlier, from Taylor's belt and slipped it into the back waistband of his jeans. "Perfect timing, by the way. Whatcha got in that bag? Bricks?"

Mackenzie raised an eyebrow. "Canned soup and tuna. I think that guy's head just dented the cans."

"I wouldn't be surprised. Remind me never to cross you again. You're a bit scary." He grinned and then moved to the first man that he'd hit with the lamp. He searched him for weapons, finding another pistol that he slipped into the front waistband of his jeans. He also pocketed the man's car keys. Neither man had a cell phone on him. "Were you able to find help?"

"No. I found another cabin down the road a bit, but it was basically empty inside except for the food. I left a note with my contact info so I could pay the people back. I don't want you arresting me for theft or anything."

Jake smiled. There were probably few people in the world who would have gone to the trouble to make sure the owners were compensated for a few dollars' worth of groceries. He liked the fact that Mackenzie was honest, even in these desperate circumstances.

"I also found something that you're going to appreciate," she said with a smile. She pulled out the Tylenol from her tote bag and offered Jake two pills and the water bottle. He downed the pills immediately, immensely grateful. She was honest and thoughtful—both good traits. He paused a moment to take her measure. Her skin was slick with sweat and her hair was mussed, but the flush in her cheeks made her even prettier, and her light blue eyes were concerned and caring. "Thanks. My head is really hurting." He handed her back the water bottle and slowly sank back down to a sitting position on the cot. The adrenaline rush was over, and his body was now protesting his exertion. He had done way too much too soon, even though he hadn't had a choice. "Do you remember seeing any plastic zip ties when you were searching this shack?"

Mackenzie squinted as if going through the contents of the cabin in her mind's eye. "No, but there is a huge amount of fishing line in one of these drawers, and I have the rope I found earlier with the mosquito netting. Will those help?"

Jake shrugged. "Couldn't hurt." He waited for her to get the supplies since she knew exactly where to look. Then he used both to tie up the hands and feet of the two criminals as he didn't have any handcuffs. He used quite a bit of fishing line on each man to guarantee they were secured. "You know, what I didn't find was a cell phone. Neither guy had one. It sure would have made our lives easier if we could have just called for help."

Mackenzie shrugged. "At least you got the car keys. That will save us from walking in this heat." She wiped her brow. "Believe me when I tell you it's hot out there."

Jake nodded. "I don't doubt it. Florida in July is no picnic, even though it's getting late." He glanced out the window. "We don't have too much sunlight left out there." He walked to the doorway, looked at the car and then returned. "Now that I've got these guys in custody, I don't want to just leave them here. But I don't think I have enough energy to drag them out to the car, and they're way too big for you. Deadweight is incredibly heavy." He reached down to grab Taylor under the arms and tried to drag him out of the shack, but even with Mackenzie's help, it was too much for him, and he felt the blood rushing in his ears. His injuries and the fighting had just taken too much out of him. Despite all of their movements, both men were still unconscious, so Jake tested the binding around their hands to make sure they were still secure.

"Yep, they're staying here. We'll send help for them once we get safely back into town." Jack took a look at the second man's features as he double-checked his bindings, but he didn't recognize him. He moved the man's face in Mackenzie's direction so she could see him.

"Do you know this guy?"

Mackenzie shook her head. "I don't know his name, but he was the one with Taylor when they brought us out here before."

Suddenly, they turned quickly toward the door as a new sound surprised them.

Someone was coming. They heard the putter of a car engine, and their eyes met.

"Now what?" Mackenzie asked, her eyes rounding.

"Outside and behind the car, just in case," Jake said quickly. He grabbed her hand and pulled her outside, and they both crouched behind the green sedan. They could hear the car getting closer, and Jake let go of Mackenzie and moved to the front fender so he could get a better look at the road. As he watched, a silver SUV slowly pulled up beside the green sedan and parked. Jake saw Derek Lager get out of the car and start walking toward the shack, followed by a petite brunette woman and another man wearing a baseball cap with the Miami Dolphins logo. He didn't recognize the other two, but Lager he would know anywhere, despite the sloppy-looking goatee that Lager had grown or the shaggy hair that now covered his collar. He was surprised that the man was personally involved in this situation, but he would have time to connect the dots once he got everyone in custody.

Jake turned and motioned for Mackenzie to stay down. He then turned back to the new arrivals. He knew he only had a few moments before they realized that their companions were out cold and trussed up like Thanksgiving turkeys. He rose slightly, using the car as a shield, and pointed his gun. "Freeze, Lager!"

Lager raised an eyebrow as he noticed Jake and his gun. He gave a smile and turned slightly. "Why, hello there, Deputy. What are you doing out here in this neck of the woods?"

"Your friends brought me out here, Lager, but I have to say, their Southern hospitality leaves a lot to be desired."

"I believe I'd have to agree with you if I knew who you were talking about, but I don't have any friends that would do such a thing." He took a step closer. "You look rather the worse for wear."

Jake shrugged. "Just a little bump on the head." He shifted his eyes between the three people, keeping a watch for any sudden movements. So far, the man in the hat and the woman had done nothing but stare at him. "Why don't you three reach out and put your hands on the SUV for me."

Lager looked as if he might be considering following Jake's directions, but a groan from inside the cabin drew his attention. He motioned with his head. "Who've you got in there?"

"The friends of yours I mentioned. One's named Bryson Taylor. Not sure of the other guy's name, but maybe you can enlighten me. Neither one of them are too happy right about now. I think they both got a small bump on the head."

Lager shook his head again. "Yeah, well, sorry, but I don't know those guys. It's too bad you're having such a rough time of it, though."

Jake was losing patience with the conversation. He raised himself up a little bit. "Hands on the SUV, Lager. You and your friends. Now."

Suddenly, the man in the hat pulled a pistol from his back waistband and fired at Jake. The shot went wild, but Jake's return shot hit the man in the shoulder. All three of the criminals dove for cover and disappeared behind the SUV, and Jake heard the wounded man groan.

"Lager, I didn't want it to go this way, but you're making it hard on yourself. Why don't you and your friends throw out your guns before someone else gets hurt?"

"Actually, Officer," Lager answered in his thick country drawl that mirrored Jake's Southern accent, "I believe we have you outnumbered. If you had any help out here, you wouldn't be hiding behind that car. I'm also sorry to say, you don't look all that well. Why don't you throw out your gun, and I promise not to kill you. If I'm feelin' charitable, I might even drop you off at the closest hospital before we go on our merry way."

"Murder isn't your game, Lager. I know you better than that. And killing a law enforcement officer in Florida carries the death penalty. Give yourself up peacefully and nobody else will get shot. You know I'm pretty good with a pistol." Jake turned and motioned for Mackenzie to stay down, go into the woods and get away from the car. The situation was quickly deteriorating, and he knew that the man in the hat, the woman and Lager could all be coming around both ends of the car at any moment for an ambush. He wasn't sure, but he imagined that all three were packing guns. He wanted to get Mackenzie out of the line of fire in case Lager decided to shoot his way out of this situation. He would have played this whole scenario differently if he had been by himself, but his first priority right now had to be keeping Mackenzie safe. She had already gotten much more than she had bargained for by being kidnapped. Now that he finally had her out of their clutches, he wanted to make sure she stayed that way. Their eyes met, and she nodded at him. Grabbing the tote bag at her feet, she crouched low and retreated into the woods. Jake called out again to cover the sound of her retreat.

"Come on, Lager. The clock is ticking. There's still time to end this now before anyone else gets hurt. Throw out your guns, and we'll talk about this." When Lager didn't answer, Jake knew instinctively that he was about to be attacked. He kept his gun ready and quickly followed the path Mackenzie had taken into the nearby stand of pines, thankful that she had retreated and was no longer in sight. Bullets followed him almost immediately, and one narrowly missed his head, sending bark flying from a nearby longleaf pine. Jake dove behind a fallen log and returned fire, catching sight of all three aggressors, who had rounded the green sedan with guns drawn just as he was entering the forest. His first shot caught the Dolphins fan in the knee, and the man screamed out in pain and fell to the ground. Lager and the woman, however, were able to take cover again behind the green sedan before his bullets could find their mark. He fired again. One bullet hit the sedan's engine and the other hit the top of the right front tire. The wheel instantly sank and tipped the car to the right. Lager returned fire, and a bullet hit the tree behind Jake; another shook the bush on his right.

Jake leaned his forehead against his hand for a moment and said a quick prayer of thanks. His head was still throbbing from the noise of the weapons and all the physical activity, but he and Mackenzie were both alive and relatively unscathed. There was a lot to be thankful for. He raised his head again and scanned the area.

He heard muffled voices but couldn't make out the words. He heard car doors open and close and also saw some movement from between the vehicles. He didn't have a shot, however, so he pulled himself to his feet and moved about ten feet to his left, using the trees as a shield. Still no shot. He moved again, silently stalking the vehicle and his quarry. Suddenly, he heard the silver SUV engine roar to life and pull away down the road in a plume of dust. He followed the SUV from the cover of the trees and aimed for another shot to disable the vehicle. There wasn't a shot worth taking, though, so he ended up securing the weapon back in his waistband. He moved cautiously toward the green sedan and the cabin but wasn't surprised to see that both of his captives had disappeared along with Lager and his friends. Lager had undoubtedly cut their bindings and gotten them both into the SUV before escaping.

Jake kicked at a nearby tree, his hands on his hips and his mouth in a scowl. He pulled out the clip on his pistol and checked his ammunition. He had three rounds left. He checked the other pistol and found another four rounds. That wasn't much if Lager decided to come back and try again. He blew out a long breath and raked his fingers through his hair, careful to avoid his injury. At least they were momentarily safe. That was something. But Jake had a very bad feeling that his problems with Derek Lager were just beginning.

FOURTEEN

Mackenzie peeked around the tree and could see Jake double-checking the shack for the two men he had tied up with fishing line. A moment later he turned and called out toward the woods.

"Mackenzie? Come on back. We're safe now. Lager and company all cleared out."

Mackenzie gingerly made her way back to the shack, being much more careful this time to avoid the blackberry brambles and other Florida foliage that she had totally ignored when she had taken refuge in the woods. Her legs felt heavy, as if she had run several miles instead of the hundred yards or so that she had actually gone into the woods. She couldn't remember ever being so scared in her entire life. Well, okay. Being kidnapped, with Bryson Taylor leering at her, had to be a close second. Today had definitely been a winner in the fear department! She had hoped for some excitement when she had started this project with the US Marshals, but today had been much more than she had bargained for. Not to mention the fact that she had already lost her apartment, her belongings and her editing equipment, and maybe even her camera.

She reached the shack and noted the missing SUV, but her immediate concern was Jake. Although he had obviously improved since she had left him the first time, she could tell he was really struggling. As if to emphasize the point, she saw him start to sway a little, and he caught himself against the side of the cabin and leaned against the wooden siding.

"Funny thing, adrenaline," he said as she approached. "I was feeling a lot better about five minutes ago."

"You mean before those people tried to kill us?" She took his arm and helped him back into the shack and over to the cot. He sat down heavily.

"You said you wanted to learn about what life's like for someone serving with the US Marshals."

She raised an eyebrow. "Are you trying to tell me this is one of your average days?"

Jake smiled. "No. It's better than most."

Mackenzie couldn't help herself. She smiled back. Somehow it was hard to remember how scared she had been or how dire their situation was when Jake was sitting there smiling at her and making her feel like everything was going to be okay. She reached into her tote bag and pulled out the soup. "I don't know about you, but I'm starving. It's not gourmet, but how about a little snack before we hit the road? I doubt they'll be returning anytime soon."

"Sounds like a plan. What else did you snag over there?"

"Tuna, and the absolutely indispensable can opener."

"Too bad I'm not in my own kitchen. I could doctor all this up and make it actually taste pretty good."

"Doctor it?" Mackenzie asked as she found a pan and opened the cans of soup.

Jake shrugged. "Cooking is one of my hobbies. I like to eat well, so I learned a few tricks in the kitchen. Adding fresh spices and a little bit of this and that can make a real difference if you're forced to eat something out of a can."

Mackenzie continued working, intrigued. For some reason, being in law enforcement and cooking were two things she had never linked together, and she didn't remember him liking to spend time in the kitchen. She was beginning to realize there was a lot she didn't know about Jake. "Back when you were in college, I remember you liked pizza a lot." She remembered once when Jake and Jonathan had sent her out to pick up a pizza and had disappeared when she returned. She had been heartbroken that they had ditched her once again, and had ended up eating half of the pie, just so they wouldn't get as much if and when they returned. She blinked away the memory. "I didn't know you liked to cook."

Jake shook his head. "It's a recent thing. I took some classes a couple of years ago that got me trying new ideas and working with foods I'd never tried. I've learned a lot."

Mackenzie laughed. "I can follow a recipe, but I'm not too creative in the kitchen. In fact, for me, cooking for one hardly makes it worth it to go to a lot of trouble."

Jake raised an eyebrow as if considering something. He was quiet for a moment and then asked, "Well, how about cooking for two? We never did finish our firearms training. Might as well grill something and make a day of it. I can whip up some steaks and sides that are guaranteed to make your taste buds sing. I'm no Iron Chef, but my team seems to like what I fix. I cook for them now and again."

Mackenzie didn't answer right away. On one hand, she was flattered by the offer, but on the other, she had promised herself to stay away from relationships to protect her heart. Even though she was attracted to Jake, anything with the deputy US marshal besides friendship seemed entirely too risky. She shrugged and continued stirring the soup but didn't turn to look at Jake.

"I'll think about it." She busied herself with washing two mugs and pouring the soup, but when she turned, she could tell that he had been studying her. His perusal sent sparks flying and caused a nervous twitter in her stomach.

"Chicken noodle, the favorite of school kids everywhere," she said with a smile, hoping to soften her ambiguous answer as she handed him the cup.

"Thanks." Jake took the cup but raised an eyebrow. "Is it me, the steaks or the firearms lesson that has you on the fence?"

Mackenzie felt her heart trip. She had hoped to change the subject but could see that Jake really wanted to know her answer. She took a drink of soup from her cup to buy some time, but Jake wasn't fooled and noticed her hesitance.

"Come on. Where's that honesty you're famous for?"

"All right. I'll give you the condensed version. The truth is, I was engaged about a year ago. We had a nasty breakup, and now I'm a bit gun-shy. Honestly, going on a date with anyone doesn't seem too wise to me."

Jake put his cup down. "I'm so sorry."

Mackenzie took another sip from her cup. "Thanks. Time is a good healer, but it doesn't make the pain go away completely." She shifted. "Anyway, although I find you very attractive, I'm not looking for another relationship. I just can't imagine putting my heart on the line like that again, even if it's just something as simple as a steak dinner. In my book, it's just too dicey."

Jake put up his hands, a hint of laughter in his eyes. "Wait a minute. You mean you have no trouble following me with a video camera as I chase down criminals that really enjoy shooting at you, but you're afraid of an afternoon of grilling in the Florida sunshine? Come on, Mackenzie. What's wrong with that picture? We already talked about this when we were discussing my horses."

Mackenzie laughed. He did have a point—albeit a small one. She looked into his eyes and tried to push away the tingles that were tickling her arms. It was as if he could see right through her. He did have very nice eyes, and she liked the way they crinkled at the corners when he smiled. He also had a nice mouth. And nice lips… She turned away so she would quit admiring his features. How could she make him understand? She wasn't even sure if she was making any sense, especially when her heart and her head were warring with each other. "I guess it all boils down to the fact that it's a different kind of risk."

A moment passed. Then another.

"And are you sure it doesn't have anything with the way I treated you in the past?"

She didn't know how to answer that one. The silence loomed.

"Look, I need to apologize to you again. I should have been there for you and your family after Jonathan died. I don't have a good excuse. All I can say is that his death really hurt, and I deal better with pain on my own. I know you tried to contact me, and I never called back. Whenever I thought about you, it seemed to make the pain of losing him even worse. It was easier to just cut off all ties with you and your family. I was selfish, and I didn't consider how his loss hurt you. I'll always be sorry for that."

She considered his words, thankful that he had explained what he had been going through after Jonathan's death. "All this time, I thought I had done something to drive you away," she said softly. "I knew I drove you crazy, and I always felt guilty."

He caught her eye, surprise in his features. "Oh, no, Mackenzie. You hadn't done anything but be kind and considerate. Losing Jonathan was like losing my right arm. I didn't know how to deal with pain like that, so I threw myself into my job and pretty much ignored everyone else. I loved him like a brother." He picked up his cup again and downed the rest of the steaming soup.

How wrong she had been. It felt good to finally let the blame slide from her shoulders. So she hadn't driven Jake away. Thinking back, she began to realize that unlike the popular kids, he had been the type to have a few good friends instead of several acquaintances. He had been quiet yet always up for a challenge—the perfect sidekick for her brother, who had been boisterous and flamboyant. She knew Jonathan's death had hurt him, but she was only beginning to understand the depth of the pain he had suffered. Everyone dealt with death in different ways. Mackenzie's way had been to surround herself with friends who could distract her and help her move on. When Jake had disappeared, she had mistaken his absence for anger or hurt that she had inadvertently caused.

She squeezed his hand. "Thank you for explaining that. It means a lot to me." She took a deep breath. "Maybe we shouldn't keep the past hidden away after all. There are a lot of wonderful things about that time that I do want to remember, and I never want to forget my brother." She nudged him playfully. "Remember that time when you and Jonathan were watching a movie over at our house, and I kept pestering you to let me watch it, too?"

He smiled. "Yeah. Jonathan put salt all over your ice cream, and you didn't know it until you took that first bite…"

She laughed. "I got him back the next day. I loosened the lid on the saltshaker, so when he tried to put some on his fries, the entire shaker opened up and salt went everywhere. He chased me down and tickled me for, like, fifteen minutes after that. It was hysterical!" She squeezed his hand again. "You know, most of the reason why I acted like such an idiot around you was because I had such a big crush on you. I thought you were the hottest guy I'd ever seen." She leaned back and took his empty mug. "I can't believe I just told you that."

She quickly stood and busied herself by washing the two mugs. She turned as she shook her hands to dry them, since she'd already used the one dish towel she'd found in the shack to clean up Jake's wound earlier. "Are you ready to blow this Popsicle stand and hit the road? I want to get going before we lose any more daylight. Like you said before, I doubt they're coming back, but I certainly don't want to test that theory."

Jake nodded. "Sure thing." He raised an eyebrow but pulled himself to his feet. Her heart was beating like a bass drum, especially after she noticed the look of admiration and interest she saw reflected in his features. She felt scared and delighted at the same time.

"Do we have any plan besides walking down that lovely country lane in search of a cell phone?" she asked.

"Nope, that's pretty much it. The green car was hit with a couple of bullets, so it's out of commission. We should just follow Lager's route and see if we can find civilization again. Hopefully we'll find someone before it gets dark."

FIFTEEN

Jake watched her clean up the dishes, her words reverberating in his head. He'd always known she'd had a crush on him when she was younger, but he had pushed her away at every opportunity. Apparently she didn't harbor the same feelings anymore. Still, if she had been attracted to him then, he could probably hope for at least a date night if he was patient. He was surprised by his desire to spend more time with her, but he couldn't deny his feelings, which were growing with each passing moment that he spent with her.

Mackenzie packed up the tuna and can opener, along with the water bottle. They still had one can left, and he agreed that it was a good idea to save it just in case they didn't find anyone who could help them anytime soon. He had no idea how long it would take them to find another human being, and he realized that his injuries would slow them down considerably.

He checked his watch and noted the time. After another hour or so, he could take some more medicine for his headache. His pain had lessened somewhat, but his body was still sending him signals that he needed to rest. *Soon*, he promised himself, and followed Mackenzie out to the road. They walked for several minutes in silence, and Jake found himself just enjoying the company. He had surprised himself with the dinner invitation, but he'd acted on the impulse before really considering the consequences. She had said she wasn't ready for a relationship, but was he? He was married to his work. In fact, he couldn't recall the last woman he had actually dated. Most of the people he dealt with were pure evil—just like Taylor and Lager. Either one would slit his throat for fifty bucks and a beer. Still, there was something about Mackenzie that pulled him toward her. She was refreshing, and the more he got to know her, the more he realized how different and special she really was. Perhaps there were some good people left in the world after all. He smiled to himself. It didn't hurt that she'd admitted she found him attractive, either.

He thought about his job and his horses, the two things that made his life satisfactory. He loved both, and his horses kept him from being lonely. Or did they? An emptiness swept over him that he hadn't expected, and he suddenly felt unwilling to examine that thought any closer. Mackenzie seemed to notice his change in demeanor and touched his arm lightly.

"Are you okay, Deputy? Do you need to rest a bit?"

Jake shook his head. It would be dark soon, and he didn't want to delay them any further. He needed to focus on something else, so he turned his attention to the case at hand. "Let's put your detective hat back on and talk through a few things as we walk. Are you game?"

"Sure thing," she agreed.

They left the building, and after a few yards, Jake started to talk. "Okay. We have two criminals involved in this crime. Case number one—we've got Carter Beckett trying to sabotage all of the copies of your homeless children video so no one will connect him to the copiers in the building. We now think, thanks to you, that the copiers were being used to steal people's personal information from the hard drives. So the question is, what was he doing with the identities he was stealing that was worth killing for?"

"What kinds of crimes has he committed in the past?" Mackenzie asked.

"He started off by committing armed robbery— both of a convenience store and of a bank in Cairo, Georgia. That's what first brought him to our attention. Bank robbery is a federal crime."

"Did he ever hurt anyone?"

Jake nodded his head. "Yes, and apparently without regret. He killed the clerk at the convenience store. I think he would have killed you too, if given the chance. Otherwise he wouldn't have been shooting at you when he was trying to eliminate all of the copies of your movie. He had to be sure you didn't recognize him, even though he was only in the background."

"So that means, whatever he's in on, it's probably much bigger than some simple identity theft. Right?"

Jake nodded. She had a point. "Right. Okay, so case number two. We've got Derek Lager. He rented the space where we found the copiers and was probably the one who actually purchased the machines. We'll know for sure once we chase the paper trail, but my guess is he's the one who hired Carter Beckett to get the information he needed from the copiers."

Mackenzie's eyes brightened, and Jake could tell she was getting excited as the pieces started to fit together in her head. "So what's his rap sheet look like again?"

"Besides being an incredibly good forger, Derek Lager is the king of fraud. He ran a huge Ponzi scheme a few years back and scored millions. He's done loan fraud, foreclosure fraud, pigeon drop scams… You name it, he's probably tried it. He's not a killer, though, which is probably why we're both alive today. If he were, I'm sure he would have chased us further into the woods and tried to finish the job." Jake stopped walking for a minute and took a breath. A small wave of nausea hit him, and he swayed on his feet.

Mackenzie noticed and caught his arm. "Let's take a break. You've been through a lot today."

He nodded and allowed her to lead him to the side of the road and sit propped up against a tree. Thoughts continued to swirl around in his mind about the case. "Okay, so let's say Beckett and Lager are partners. Lager is the brains behind the operation, and Beckett is the worker bee. Since Beckett and Taylor are chums, Beckett brings in Taylor, who becomes another worker bee."

"Right. And my film is a threat because it links Beckett to the building and the copy machines, so they tried to eliminate both me and the copies of the movie before someone somewhere saw my documentary and made the connection, which would somehow bring down their operation."

"Right." Jake agreed. "Although, I don't think Lager or Taylor made the connection between you and the film, at least initially. If they had, I think we would have both been killed at the shack." He paused and rubbed his head absently. "So we're down to two questions. Number one, what kind of scheme is Lager involved in with the information he is stealing, and number two, how exactly is Bryson Taylor involved?"

"It's too bad no one was able to get Beckett to confess during the interrogations."

Jake nodded. "Yeah, he screamed 'lawyer' as soon as we got him back behind bars. He'll still go down for his priors, but we really don't have anything that connects him to Lager yet that's concrete, or Taylor for that matter. I mean, we know he's in your video, and we arrested him with a firearm in the building where Lager was renting space, but that's all circumstantial. Everything right now is guesswork."

Mackenzie sat silently for a few minutes. "Do you think Beckett's appearance in my film is really enough to kill over? I mean, who really would have noticed that he was in the background besides someone who was involved with law enforcement like you? And do you really think that you or someone like you would actually watch my homeless children video and see him in the background?"

Jake shrugged. "Beckett is an extremely careful man. There's a reason why he was on the most-wanted list. He doesn't make a lot of mistakes. In his mind, it was probably better to eliminate the threat before it became a problem, rather than waiting to see if anyone actually made the connection."

Mackenzie's eyes rounded. "So what happens when Lager realizes his mistake and he missed his opportunity to kill me at the cabin?"

Jake squeezed her arm. "I think he'll want to finish the job, but as I said, he's usually not a killer. I wouldn't put it past him to hire someone, though. My guess is, he'll send Taylor after you and the other copies of your movie, and if Taylor fails, he'll hire another flunky to do the job until he knows the threat is neutralized. We definitely need to keep you in protective custody until we've got Lager behind bars and we figure out his entire scheme and how these pieces all fit together. Otherwise, you're still in constant danger." He stood and brushed the sand from his pants. "Ready to go? I'm feeling a bit better."

Mackenzie joined him, and they continued down the road in silence for a bit. Jake could tell that Mackenzie was still putting all the information together in her mind. After a few minutes, she spoke up again. "Well, since Taylor doesn't know my true identity, it still makes sense that Lager was probably just keeping us under wraps so they'd have enough time to move things from a warehouse and cut their losses. Sounds like some sort of stolen property to me." Her voice filled with a new level of enthusiasm. "So maybe Taylor has been in on this since the beginning and is the third man in the ring. Lager is the brains, Beckett did the work with the copiers and Taylor is the one in charge of storing some sort of stolen merchandise. And we're one step ahead of them since we know the three are working together."

"True, but we still don't know their scheme or the extent of it. And we need to keep you safe in the meantime. Like I said before, Lager doesn't like loose ends."

"But by now, he knows about Beckett's arrest and he knows my movie implicated Beckett, not Lager. Yet they sent someone to my hotel. Why would he still care?"

Her words were cut short as Jake grabbed her arm and pulled her quickly behind some trees. "There's a car coming down the road. Let's hope it's a friend and not Lager or one of his team."

Mackenzie's face paled and he took her hand to reassure her. "Don't worry. We'll stay hidden until we can tell whether it's friend or foe. If anything happens to me, you wait until you know you're safe, and then just keep walking until you find a phone. Call my team at the office. They'll know what to do." He squeezed her hand and then turned back to the road, hoping that the oncoming vehicle was driven by a friendly fisherman instead of a gun-toting member of the Lager team.

SIXTEEN

A plume of smoke obscured the vehicle for a few minutes, but as the dust cleared, Mackenzie's heart began to beat frantically against her chest. It was the silver SUV, and that could mean only one thing. Taylor must have regained consciousness and told Lager about the woman he had abducted. Lager had put two and two together and realized that Mackenzie was the videographer they had been trying to kill, and they had let her escape. Now they were coming back to finish the job. Jake realized the threat as well and pulled her closer to the ground, shielding them from the road behind a group of palmetto palms. Their eyes met, and she found comfort there despite the dire circumstances. He was still holding her hand, and she gripped his tightly, willing her hands to stop shaking. The vehicle was driving slowly, and with each second that passed she grew more convinced that their hiding place was about to be discovered. The vehicle stopped and she gasped, but Jake shook his head.

"Easy, Mackenzie. It's okay," he whispered.

She nodded at him and squeezed his hand even

tighter. Another minute passed. Then another. She could hear the rumbling of the engine only a few feet away, and she closed her eyes, praying fervently. Suddenly, the vehicle engine wined, and the SUV started off again, heading back toward the shack. Jake motioned for her to stay down a few moments longer, and she happily complied. They waited a full five minutes before Jake finally stood and helped her to her feet.

"Are you okay?" he asked gently as he wiped some of the sand off her cheek.

She didn't answer him right away, and he must have realized just how shaken up she was after seeing the SUV. He didn't hesitate. He wrapped his arms around her and just held her for a moment as she composed herself. She accepted the hug with gratitude and enjoyed the support and strength he offered in his simple embrace. She rested her head against his shoulder and closed her eyes for a moment. It had been such a harrowing day. Who was she kidding? It had been a traumatic week! She was beginning to wonder if she would ever feel safe again. Maybe she wasn't invincible after all. Jake's arms were comforting, and for several minutes, she just stood there, accepting his help. Finally, she pulled back slightly, and he gently released her. Their eyes met, and she gave him a tentative smile.

"Thanks, Jake. Sorry I lost it."

He smiled back, and she noticed a dimple appear on his right cheek. His expression instantly made her feel better. "I think you're entitled to stop and take a breath. It has been a crazy week for you." He took her hand and led her back to the road. "You're amazing, did you know that?" He didn't wait for an answer and instead glanced up and down the road, making sure the vehicle was nowhere in sight before stepping back onto the easement.

They walked in silence for several minutes, and even though Jake still held her hand, she didn't pull away. His touch was comforting, and she welcomed the contact. After about another mile or so, Mackenzie saw another driveway in the distance, and she encouraged Jake to follow her as she turned off the main road. She didn't know if there were people at the end of the driveway or even a house, but she'd noticed that Jake was starting to sway a bit on his feet and his gait had slowed considerably. He had to be tired, especially since he was fighting against the concussion and other injuries he had sustained. She was surprised that he was even on his feet at all. Twilight had also fallen, and if they didn't find help soon, they would end up walking in the dark, which didn't seem like the wise thing to do.

They came upon a house that was similar in size and style to the one where she had found the soup, but unfortunately, this house also seemed to be abandoned for the summer months. Although they tried the doors and windows, all were locked tightly. She didn't find a hidden key this time, but Jake noticed that the back door had several small glass panes, so he broke the one closest to the door lock, grinning sheepishly as Mackenzie raised an eyebrow.

"Don't worry. I'll leave a note and pay them back."

She laughed and followed him in. Unfortunately,

the electricity was turned off, so when she tried the light switch, nothing happened.

"No phone," Jake added after doing a search of the small building. There was still a little light coming in the windows, but there was no moon tonight. It was getting dark fast, so Mackenzie went to a couple of the windows and opened the shades, hoping to use the available light as long as possible. Although it looked like a small bungalow from the outside, the inside resembled more of an art studio, and the one bedroom had no bed but was instead filled with art supplies, half-finished canvases and tubes of various colors of paint. It did have a recliner, though, and a couple of tables, but that was the extent of the furniture. There was no food in the kitchen, but the water was turned on, which meant they were able to use the bathroom, wash up a bit and drink full glasses of cool water to help them stay hydrated.

Mackenzie found another first aid kit and asked Jake to sit at the small kitchen table so she could change the bandages on his head wound. He did as she asked, and she carefully pulled off the soiled gauze, dabbed the cut with a clean cloth and bandaged him again. She tried to be gentle with her ministrations, but she could tell he was still in a great deal of pain. After she was finished, she got him another glass of water and more pain medicine.

"So where did you learn your first aid skills?" Jake asked quietly.

"Girl Scouts," she answered with a wink. "Believe it or not, we actually did a lot more than sell cookies in my troop. I earned a heap of badges." She finished up and patted him on the shoulder. "Okay, you're good to go."

He stood, and they walked the short distance to the living room. It was small and contained only a large couch and a couple of nice wooden shelves packed with books. A throw rug decorated the floor, and there was an end table and small lamp nearby. Several embroidered pillows decorated the couch.

Mackenzie moved to the couch and sat down wearily. The stress had made her more tired than she realized. "You know, I usually go to sleep much later than this, but today I can't seem to keep my eyes open."

Jake removed both guns from his waistband and set them on the nearby end table. He then stretched a bit, apparently unsure of what to do next. He finally broke the silence. "Look, we don't have a lot of options here. You sleep on the couch, and I'll take the floor." He started to lower himself to the small rug, but Mackenzie jumped to her feet and stopped him, kicking herself for not being more sensitive.

"Oh, no, you don't. I'm sorry I wasn't thinking. You're the one with the concussion, remember? You take the couch. I'll take the recliner in the bedroom."

Jake shook his head and then winced. He was about to speak but Mackenzie reached over and took his hand and pulled him over to the couch. He resisted and they ended up standing toe to toe in front of the couch, neither budging.

"Look, I'm no Boy Scout, but I was raised with manners. What kind of Southern gentleman would I be if I made you sleep on that old lumpy chair? Plus, you'll be in a different room. I want you close by in case danger comes knocking. I'll be worried about you all night if you're in there. The guilt and stress would make it impossible for me to sleep." His slow Southern twang seemed to accent the point, and Mackenzie couldn't help herself. She laughed.

"Okay. I've duly noted that chivalry isn't dead. Now can we just agree that you're injured, and I'm *choosing* to sleep on that recliner? It doesn't look so bad. And it's not like this house is that big. I won't be that far away. I'll be fine, I promise." She gently pushed him down to a sitting position on the couch and then grabbed one of the pillows. "Okay if I take one of these?"

He nodded and leaned back, clearly exhausted. Mackenzie was amazed at his fortitude. He'd been through quite a lot today and had still managed to walk several miles and keep her safe in the process. She wondered if anyone had ever really showed their appreciation to this man for everything he did to make the world a better place. Law enforcement personnel led dangerous lives. Yet they didn't get paid much and usually had to deal with the worst of the worst in society. She didn't think she had really appreciated him herself until this exact moment, and she silently vowed to make sure her movie about the US Marshals showed not only the work they did but also their strength of character and unstoppable resolve. It was inspiring, as well it should be. She reached across the space, squeezed his hand and then released it. "Rest easy, Jake. And thank you for everything you did today. I'm alive and well because of you."

"You're welcome. We'll get through this, okay? Don't worry."

"I'm not worried," she answered. "I've got you."

Jake paused a moment and had a strange look on his face, but the darkness masked his features and it was really hard to tell what he was thinking. For a moment she thought he was going to say something else, but in the end he shrugged and stretched out on the couch, his eyes closing almost the minute his head hit the pillow.

Jake awoke slowly hours later, a feeling of content-ment washing over him, despite the fact that he was still extremely sore in several places. He blinked his eyes, suddenly remembering where he was and what had happened the day before as he glanced around the shadow-filled room. His brain seemed clearer, and he was immensely grateful that he'd had an opportunity to rest. It was still dark outside, and when he moved his arm to reach for his watch, he realized the source of his contentment. Mackenzie was only a short dis-tance from him, and he liked the idea that she was nearby. He stood and stretched. Then he went over to the bedroom door and opened it softly. He couldn't see much, but he could tell that she was still sleeping on the recliner. She was curled up like a cat, and he could hear her soft, even breathing. He was glad she was able to get some well-deserved rest.

When he was with Mackenzie, it was a little harder to remember how nasty the criminals were and a little harder to convince himself that there were no good people left in the world. In fact, now that she had come into his life, there was a small light where before it had only been darkness. He said a short prayer of thanks, grateful that God had sent her. Perhaps that was the secret—he needed to be thankful for the blessings in his life instead of dwelling so much on the negative.

Despite all that they had been through, the faint smell of jasmine wafted over him. How did she manage to smell so good? It was no wonder she didn't want to go out with him. He grimaced and then turned back toward the couch. He was gristly and bitter, but for this moment, he was going to enjoy having her near and imagine a world where people cared about each other and she was willing to be in his life to share the good and bad that each day brought.

Suddenly, a bright light from outside shone across his eyes, and he saw headlights flash against the trees outside the window. A few seconds later, he could hear the motor of a car coming closer to the house. He quickly returned to the bedroom and nudged Mackenzie, trying not to startle her too much but also wanting to spur her into action.

"Mackenzie, someone is coming. We need to get out of here."

"What?" Her voice was sleepy, and she yawned and stretched.

He took her hands and gently pulled her to her feet and started leading her toward the kitchen and the back door. He realized they had precious little time to find a hiding place before the occupants of the vehicle were upon them. "We need to get out of here. Somebody just drove up to the house. We're in danger."

The word *danger* must have startled her because he saw her eyes widen. She was instantly awake and ready to follow him. She only paused a moment to stop and pick up the tote bag while he secured the two guns back in his waistband, and then they were out and down the steps of the back porch and into the safety of the surrounding woods.

Jake was glad that Mackenzie was awake enough to immediately assess the peril and follow him without question. They silently moved behind the trees and continued until they were about forty feet away from the house. Suddenly, they heard car doors close, and they quickly ducked down below the nearby foliage. A moment later, they saw two men circling the house. Both were carrying flashlights and there was just enough light to get a look at their faces. He didn't recognize the man who wore a Gators hat, but the other was Taylor. Jake heard Mackenzie gasp. She instantly covered her mouth with her hand, but Taylor seemed to have heard the small noise and stopped. He swung his flashlight around and aimed it toward the woods.

Jake felt his adrenaline surge, and a wave of protectiveness swept over him. Knowing that his movement was hidden by the tree, he slowly moved his hand to her arm and gave her a gentle squeeze of comfort. He could feel her trembling and wanted to reassure her. She had to be terrified.

The flashlight beam slowly flashed around them, but apparently Taylor didn't see anything. After a few more sweeps, he aimed the light back at the house, and he and the man in the hat went inside.

Jake took the opportunity to take Mackenzie's hand and lead her farther into the woods. It was hard to see, but if Taylor saw anything in the house that revealed their presence, Jake knew his next move would be to start searching the woods surrounding the house. He still had both guns, but he had limited ammunition, and more important, he didn't want a gun battle with Mackenzie caught in the middle. Right now, his primary objective was keeping her safe.

She suddenly stumbled, and he helped her regain her balance. "Are you okay?" His voice was barely above a whisper, but she nodded and continued following him. After they'd zigzagged through the trees and put more distance between them and the house, Jake motioned for her to stop, and they rested a bit, sitting and leaning against a large live oak tree trunk. His head was still hurting, and he downed a couple of pain relievers although his stomach was empty. The sun was barely tipping over the horizon, and a fine mist of fog helped camouflage their location. It would have been almost pretty if they hadn't been in such danger. Pinks and oranges dotted the sky, promising a beautiful sunny day.

"Wanna break open the tuna?" Mackenzie asked softly. "I'm starving."

Jake nodded. "Sure. I just took that medicine, so it would be good to have some food, as well."

Mackenzie used the can opener and held the tuna out to him. Jake ate his share, thankful for the meal. It wasn't much, but it was far better than nothing. He handed it back and watched her finish off the can.

"I don't really like fish, but I must be really hungry because that didn't taste half bad."

Jake raised an eyebrow. "You live in Florida, but you don't eat seafood?"

Mackenzie nodded. "Guilty. I could even go vegetarian if push came to shove, but I do like chicken and a good steak now and then."

Was she sending him a message by that comment? He couldn't tell for sure, but there was a smile in her eyes. He decided to ask her out again. The worst that could happen was that she would refuse him. It was worth a try. "Does that mean you've reconsidered my offer for a good steak dinner?" He busied himself with brushing the sand off his pants, hoping that if she couldn't see his face too well, she wouldn't see the disappointment he would feel if she turned him down a second time.

"I think I'd like that."

His eyes snapped up, and he smiled. "I think I would, too." He stood before he could analyze what was happening between them. He didn't want to overthink it, but he couldn't help the sense of happiness that swept over him or the anticipation that was already tightening in his chest.

"Let's see if we can't find another road to follow."

"Deal."

They walked through the trees for another hour or so, hearing nothing but the buzzing of insects and birds chirping around them. The sun continued to rise and light their path, but they didn't come across any other houses. Finally, they came across a road, and Jake was hopeful when he saw well-worn ruts and new tire tracks in the dirt.

The sound of a vehicle startled them both, and Jake pulled Mackenzie quickly behind a copse of trees, well away from the road. The car was moving slowly, but as it approached, Jake was able to tell that it was a red Camry, which an older woman seemed to be driving. Once the car got even closer, he could tell that the woman was alone. He stepped from behind the trees and held up his badge with one hand and motioned for her to stop with the other. She slowed and eventually stopped right beside him.

"Is there a problem, Officer? You've got blood on you." The woman's eyes were large, and he could see the fear radiate across her face as she noticed his wound and blood-soaked shirt.

"Well, ma'am, I'm a deputy marshal, and my friend and I were attacked out here a few hours ago. They stole my phone, and we've been walking down this road trying to find help. Would you mind giving us a ride to the nearest phone or police station? We'd sure be grateful for your assistance."

For once in his life, Jake was thankful for his Southern accent. As he spoke, the words seemed to calm the driver considerably, and he could tell that it was his accent—and not his words—that were reassuring her. He motioned for Mackenzie to join him, and she came up to his side and smiled at the woman.

"Attacked? Oh, my. Are those bad people still around?"

Jake shook his head. "Oh, no, ma'am. They've been gone for quite a while, but they left us without any transportation. I just need to call my office, and help will be on the way." He paused. "Look, if you'd just let me borrow your phone, I could call my office, and they could send someone to pick us up."

The woman scrunched her face. "I don't have a cell phone. Bothersome little things. I don't like them." The woman's fears seemed to have dissipated somewhat, but she was still staring at the blood on his shirt. "Is that a real badge, young man?"

"Yes, ma'am. It surely is. If you want, you can drive us straight to the police station and forget the phone. They'll be happy to verify our story, and you'd really be helping us out." He smiled. "Or, if you'd rather, a hospital would be just as good. I have to get this wound taken care of as soon as I can."

The driver finally assented, and shortly they were in her car, heading out of the woods. Their problems were solved temporarily, but Jake knew that Mackenzie wouldn't be safe until Lager's schemes were exposed. Jake was anxious to find out the rest of the story and put both Lager and Taylor behind bars, where they both belonged.

SEVENTEEN

"Ready?" Mackenzie asked, her hand wrapped around the TV remote. She glanced around Jake's living room and got a thumbs-up sign from Chris and an encouraging smile from Whitney. Suddenly, Dominic entered the room, a large grin on his face. He was holding two gift bags, one pink and one blue.

"Before we get started, I just have a little gift for Jake and Mackenzie, our wayward deputy marshal and videographer." Chris and Whitney clapped and laughed. Jake, who was standing by the kitchen door frame holding a bowl of popcorn, raised an eyebrow, apparently not sure what to expect.

Dominic handed one of the bags to Jake and another to Mackenzie. "Just in case you decide to go hiking in the woods again, we all chipped in and bought you a few items to make your trip more memorable."

Mackenzie peeked inside and started laughing. She reached into the bag and pulled out a fitness activity watch, a power bar and a compass. A little deeper in the bag, she also found a small can of tuna.

"You guys are too much," she said jovially as she put on the watch. She looked over at Jake, who had also donned his new timepiece. Apparently, they had both been preprogrammed and were ready to start tracking their activities. He shook his head with a laugh and then reached over and punched Dominic in the arm. He also pulled out the power bar and compass, but instead of tuna, he found a stack of bandages at the bottom of his bag. He pulled those out and handed them back to Dominic. "You'd better hang on to these. You might need them yourself someday."

Dominic laughed. "Not hardly. When I go hiking, I don't get lost in the woods…"

Jake threw a handful of popcorn at Dominic and then handed Mackenzie the rest of the bowl as he sat down beside her on the couch. "All right, folks. Thanks for the gifts. Now let's take a look at this movie." The doctors had released Jake from the hospital after a night of observation and a few tests, and meanwhile, his team had resumed taking turns guarding her at Jake's house. They all agreed that she was still in imminent danger from Lager and his group and that Lager would probably step up his attempts to eliminate her since the US Marshals had found the copy machines, discovered the links to Taylor and the warehouse, and were investigating the entire operation. Based on what Taylor had said during the abduction, Lager's team was apparently on some sort of time frame, so it was imperative that Jake and his team quickly figured out what was going on before the evidence disappeared completely.

The group had been talking through various theories about the case with her almost constantly since breakfast, and she had enjoyed getting to know them a bit better. The conversations had been lively and had also given her fresh insight into how to make her movie an even better representation of them and the work they did. Her admiration for them had grown exponentially, and although the time in the woods had been terrifying, it had also been a great way to introduce her to the agency's work firsthand and fill her with inspiration.

Jake had returned right after lunchtime and appeared to be well on his way to recovery. The doctors had been able to use skin adhesives to close his head wound, and although he still had a variety of bruises and scrapes, his demeanor was good. He had obviously regained his energy and strength of purpose. He had been ordered to rest, but Mackenzie could tell that his injuries weren't going to slow him down in his zeal for solving this case.

He handed her a glass of ice water to go with the popcorn. "What you said as we were walking down the road made a lot of sense and really got me thinking. Someone shot that maid and damaged your hotel room *after* we had Beckett in custody. That means, even though they knew we had made the connection between your film and Beckett, they still wanted to harm you and get their hands on the remaining copies of your films. It also means we missed something. I'm hoping that if we all watch your homeless children movie a few more times, we'll catch whatever it is, which will give us a new lead in the case."

Mackenzie smiled. "I'm game if you are. And as

you're watching, if you see something that you think will improve the US Marshals video, don't be shy. I'm always open to a new perspective or idea."

Jake nudged her. "Be careful what you ask for. This team is *never* shy about giving their opinions." His comment was met by several groans and denials, and Dominic even threw a handful of popcorn at him.

They turned on the movie and didn't see anything relevant until Mackenzie stopped it and showed everyone where they had seen Beckett in the background. They watched about ten more minutes of the movie before Dominic asked her to stop it again. There were two men in the background now as another teenager was getting interviewed. It was hard to recognize the faces, but once they blew up the image, they could tell one of the men was Lager. The identity of the other person remained a mystery. After a few minutes, another unidentified man went into the building Lager had exited only moments before. "I was doing interviews at the various homeless shelters around town, which are located in low-rent districts," Mackenzie explained. "Apparently, Lager works in those buildings. These two sections of footage were taken on different days and in different locations, so he must be storing his merchandise in less expensive areas of the city."

Jake leaned forward. "I can't believe we missed this. We must have stopped the film too soon last time." He ran his fingers through his hair, avoiding his injury, before pushing on. "What if Lager is running a new instant credit fraud scheme? He gets the personal info he needs from the copiers and then makes fake driver's licenses. He gives them to his associates, who use the counterfeit licenses to apply for instant credit accounts. Then they go out and buy big-ticket items like flat-screen TVs, jewelry, laptops and the like. He has to store the merchandise somewhere, right?"

Whitney snapped her fingers. "Enter Bryson Taylor and his warehouse buddies. They store the merchandise and hang on to it until Lager finds a buyer. They resell the stuff for about half the retail value and then pocket the cash."

Jake leaned forward. "They probably even have someone choosing the identity theft victims based on their credit scores. It's easy enough to look up the victims and see whose identity is worth stealing and whose isn't. Also, I'm sure these men coming in to meet with Lager in the documentary are his buyers. He must have seen you filming and wants the movie destroyed so his buyers won't jump ship and get the merchandise from a different supplier. Without the movie, there's probably very little that ties these buyers to Lager."

"So how do we stop them?" Mackenzie asked.

"We start by going after these buyers. Let's take a closer look and run them through our facial recognition software. Once we figure out who they are, we start digging into their finances to see if we can link them to Lager."

"That still doesn't seem like enough to kill over," Mackenzie said softly. "Maybe we should watch the rest of the movie as well, just in case there's even more that we're missing."

The deputies agreed, and they all leaned back to watch the rest of the film. They didn't see anything else that looked suspicious, so after watching the entire thing a second time, Mackenzie turned it off and turned to the group. "Some of the kids I interviewed were pretty vague about how they were earning enough money to eat. I mean, I really listened to their comments that time through the movie, and the interviews made me start wondering. What if some of the older kids are working for Lager, too? What if we've stumbled upon something even bigger here?"

Jake nodded slowly. "If they look believable enough, Lager could be using them as the ones that actually take the fake licenses into the stores, apply for the credit accounts and make the purchases. Those kids would probably do the crime for barely any compensation. I mean, they're living in poverty, right? A hundred bucks to them would be a fortune."

When Mackenzie nodded, he pushed forward. "If Lager is using the homeless and poor to get the fake credit accounts, then we've stumbled upon something even bigger than I originally thought. Even though he's not normally a killer, I can see Lager coming after you to make sure that both you and your movies get destroyed. He must have seen you filming or talked to some of homeless and heard about your production. This movie could destroy his entire enterprise, not to mention putting his buyers at risk. We're talking hundreds of thousands of dollars. Maybe even more."

There was a light of excitement in his eyes and he gently put his hands on both sides of her head and met her eyes. "I think you figured it out, Mackenzie. We're going to make a detective of you yet."

Electricity sizzled between them and for a moment, the room seemed empty but for the two of them. Jake leaned a bit closer, and Mackenzie wondered if he was going to kiss her, right there in front of the team. Their eyes met, and Mackenzie actually found herself leaning closer in anticipation. The excitement of the moment had her yearning for a kiss, despite the group of witnesses.

Dominic cleared his throat, obviously uncomfortable, yet with a smile on his face. "Ah, okay then. I think it's time we spent some time on the computer, finding out how much of this we can actually prove." He stood and left the living room, followed by Whitney and Chris.

Jake suddenly noticed their departure and let his hands drop, even though his eyes never left Mackenzie's face. He could feel the excitement in the air. He hadn't been looking for a woman in his life, but suddenly, Mackenzie was sitting right in front of him, her lips parted. He moved forward a few small inches and placed a kiss on those beautiful lips. They were soft and sweet, just as he had anticipated.

Mackenzie responded and raised her hands to gently touch his cheek. The movement warmed him from the inside out and made him feel both special and cherished at the same time. He moved to kiss her again, but before he could do so, she pulled back, her eyes filled with wonder and consternation at the same time.

"So how do we catch these guys?" Mackenzie asked, her eyes finally breaking contact. She suddenly stood and moved a few feet away, as if distance could erase the feelings that were bubbling between them. Her hands moved nervously, and she ended up crossing her arms as if protecting herself from unwanted emotions.

Jake just sat there for a minute, still surprised by the feelings of attraction he was sensing. He hadn't been looking for a relationship, but he could no longer deny the feelings growing inside of him. He tilted his head a bit and studied her. She was definitely attractive, and he suddenly remembered the excitement that had radiated from her countenance when she had removed the door hinges in the shack. The memory made him laugh in delight.

"What?" Her brows drew together in question.

"Oh, nothing. I was just remembering how you got us out of that shack in the woods." Jake shook his head as if that would erase the sentiments he was discovering.

"So, I was thinking the best way to catch these guys would be to use me as bait. They want me and my movies. Why not use the media to advertise that I'm back and my movie on the homeless is about to be released for the premiere viewing at a certain place and time? They'll want to be there to stop it and stop me. You guys wait in the wings, and we take them all down in one fell swoop."

Jake stood abruptly and put his hands on his hips. Was this woman crazy? "There is no way I'm using you as bait, Mackenzie. It's too dangerous. It's amazing you're still alive as it is."

Mackenzie matched his stance. "Look, it makes sense, don't you think? We've found one of their warehouse sites but don't have any idea where they are stashing the rest of the merchandise, and like the bad guy said, time is of the essence. They wanted us out of the way so they could move the goods in the next day or two. If we don't move fast, we'll lose our opportunity and the evidence will disappear. Without more, all we have right now is conjecture. We need proof and maybe a confession or two to bring this fraud ring down."

She was making sense, but he didn't want to admit it. After just discovering his feelings for her, the last thing he wanted to do was put her back in the line of fire. True, he had no idea if the feelings would develop into something more, but his basic urge to protect her didn't waver. He hedged, not wanting to make her mad, but also not wanting to agree to put her in danger. "We'll think about it as a last resort. First, we'll do some legwork and see if we can make the arrest a different way."

Mackenzie raised an eyebrow but must have decided not to argue. Instead, she dropped her arms and shrugged. "Okay. You win. What can I do to help?"

"Open your laptop," Jake said with a smile. "And see if you can help us discover who the buyers are and where they're hiding the rest of the merchandise."

Mackenzie's head was spinning with ideas as she watched Jake go back to his desk. The team of deputy marshals had great theories but still no proof of illegal activity that they could use to stop the monstrous fraud that they had stumbled upon. Sure, they could arrest Taylor for kidnapping and battery once they caught him, but Lager was the one they wanted—the mastermind of the entire scheme.

She thought back to her video and the interviews she had just watched. Maybe the key was really with the kids themselves. She pulled out her laptop and attached the hard drive with her files. She then sorted through them until she found her notes on the various kids that had appeared on film. Despite their troubled lives, every one of the kids she had met had always carried a cell phone. Most were just pay-as-you-go phones with untraceable numbers, and she was sure that many of the numbers she had were no longer valid, yet if she could convince one of the kids to talk to her, she might be able to get the evidence she needed to blow this case wide-open.

She glanced at Jake again. He had buried himself behind his computer screen and was again swamped with paperwork and lost in his sea of forms. Her secure cell phone had been destroyed by Taylor, so she grabbed Jake's cordless house phone off the hook and disappeared back into her room with her computer and the files. It was time to make some calls and see if she could make a break in this case.

EIGHTEEN

"Max?" Mackenzie peered down the alley, but the shadows didn't reveal her quarry and a shiver of apprehension swept down her spine. She checked the fitness activity watch that Jake's team had given her. It was the right time and place, but she didn't see the homeless teenager anywhere. Had she made a mistake? She'd only been able to find one of the kids she'd interviewed for the movie, and Max, the seventeen-year-old who had been willing to meet with her, had imposed strict conditions. He would only meet with her if she came alone and only if he got to name the time and place. She had wanted to tell Jake about the meeting, but in the end had opted not to. There was no way he would have agreed to let her go, yet she was convinced that talking to Max was the only way she could make headway in this case. Jake had already made it clear he was against anything that might put her in the slightest danger, but she hadn't anticipated any problems when she'd set this meeting up or when she'd snuck away from Jake's house through the bedroom window and borrowed his car for the trek into the western side of town. Now, though, since she was alone in the alley, she was beginning to have second thoughts.

She took a few more steps. "Max?"

A skinny young man suddenly stepped out from behind a dumpster. He was wearing threadbare jeans, a black T-shirt with an advertisement for a local car repair shop and a dirty red baseball cap. He pushed some buttons on his phone and then stuck it in his pocket as he looked around nervously.

"Hey, Ms. Weaver."

Mackenzie smiled, hoping to put him at ease. She didn't remember him being this jumpy when she had met with him before, but his life wasn't an easy one, and there was no telling what had transpired since she had interviewed him. Her notes had reminded her that Max's parents had abandoned him at the local bus station, but he hadn't liked his foster parents and had run away at about the age of twelve or so. He'd been on the streets ever since.

"Hey, Max. It's good to see you."

He tilted his head and scratched at his neck. His movements were still jumpy, and she speculated again at the cause. "So what do you wanna talk about this time? I thought you finished your movie."

"I did," Mackenzie confirmed, "but I've been working with the US Marshals on a case that I think you might be involved with, and I'm wondering if you can help me figure out some of the missing pieces. Will you help me?"

Max shrugged. "Sure thing, but ah…do you have any cash?"

Mackenzie laughed to herself. Max had always been about the money, but she understood and didn't hesitate. She pulled out forty dollars and handed it to him. He quickly pocketed the money she held out but then took a few steps back. "Do you know a man named Derek Lager? He's about average height and has brown hair. He makes driver's licenses and other documents on the side."

Max rubbed his ear. Apparently he couldn't keep his hands still, and he kept looking around behind him.

"Are you expecting someone to join us?" Mackenzie asked, alarm once again making her edgy. Maybe it really hadn't been a good idea to come here on her own, despite Max's demands.

"Nah," Max said softly. He met her eyes. "I've heard of Lager. He's around sometimes."

"I'm around, too, princess." The new voice came from behind her, and despite her shock, Mackenzie instantly recognized Taylor's raspy tones. Before she could even react, Taylor grabbed her arm and pulled her around. "Well, what do you know? I knew you'd miss me and come lookin'."

Mackenzie tried to pull away, but Taylor's grip only got tighter and more painful. At the same time she struggled, Taylor pulled a hundred-dollar bill out of the front pocket of his jeans and handed it to Max. "Good work, kid."

Max had sold her out? She was surprised but then realized she shouldn't have been. A hundred bucks to a hungry street kid was like gold. The money meant he would eat tonight—and probably even for a few more days to come.

"You're not gonna hurt her, are you?" Max's eyes had rounded when Taylor grabbed her, but despite his question, she could see that Max was already backing away from them and trying to keep his distance from Taylor's grasp.

"Worry about your own life, not hers," Taylor warned.

"You know we have to take care of them both, don't you?" A new voice joined the mix, and Mackenzie saw Derek Lager himself step up from behind Max. He was holding a pistol and pointing it at Max's head. Max's faced turned an ashen white, and he held up his hands. In his haste to get away, he bumped clumsily into the dumpster and tried frantically to shake the hair out of his eyes.

"I won't tell anybody anything," the boy pleaded. "I promise."

Lager drew his lips together into a thin line. "Well, you know, Max, I'd love to believe you, but here you are, agreeing to meet with this woman and ready to spill your guts. After today, I just don't think I can trust you anymore."

"I wasn't gonna tell her anything. I was just gonna take her money. That's it."

"Sorry, but like I said, I just don't believe you," Lager responded. He pulled a zip tie out of his pocket and threw it on the ground in front of Mackenzie. "Put that around his wrists and tighten it. If you don't, I'll just shoot you right now." He waved the gun in Mackenzie's direction, and she jerked her arms away from Taylor's grasp, quickly grabbed the tie and secured the boy's wrists.

"Your turn, princess," Taylor said with a laugh. He took a step toward her and pushed her so hard that she fell on the pavement.

Pulling a zip tie from his own pocket, he bent down to secure her wrists and then roughly pulled her to her feet again. She could feel the plastic biting into her skin, but fear was coursing through her so frantically that she barely noticed. She was going to die today. There was no doubt.

Taylor moved his hands to her arms and pulled her so close that she could feel the man's heated breath on her face.

"I'm going to enjoy this," he said softly. She grimaced and turned away, but he just laughed and shifted, pulling her along with him and heading out of the alley. When they got to the street, they passed Jake's car and went to the silver SUV that was parked behind it. Taylor forced her in the back seat, and Lager did the same with Max. Then Taylor got in the driver's side, and Lager took the other front seat.

Mackenzie looked up and down the street, frantically searching for another live soul, but there was nobody around to witness their abduction. A couple of cars were driving by on a nearby crossroad, but they were too far away for Mackenzie to try to signal for help. She glanced over at Max, whose skin was still a pasty white. He was looking down and had instantly scrunched against the car door once he was inside. She turned back to see Lager and Taylor laughing at something Lager has said and wondered fleetingly if she would even survive the afternoon. It didn't look good. She started to pray.

Jake stomped impatiently, waiting for Dominic to pull up the app on his phone. His hands were on his hips, and he found it hard to even stand still. How could she have snuck out on him like that? Didn't she realize the danger?

Apparently not, he chided himself.

"I've almost got it," Dominic answered as he keyed in a few more numbers.

"And you're sure that fitness watch had a GPS and you can track her with it?" Jake asked again for the fifth time.

"Yes, Jake. Just give me a minute."

"I'm not sure she's got one. Mackenzie could be dead already for all I know." Jake had been furious when he'd discovered that Mackenzie was missing, but Dominic had quickly reassured him that they could find her rather quickly with the GPS coordinates of the fitness activity watch she was wearing. Although the GPS feature had originally been part of the joke, Jake was ecstatic that they actually had a way to find Mackenzie after she pulled her disappearing act. What he didn't have was patience to wait while Dominic fiddled with the app. He didn't know where she'd gone, but he knew it had to involve the case, and he sensed that she was in danger. The fear that gripped him was nearly debilitating.

"Okay. Got it." Dominic showed Jake a blinking dot on a map. "Looks like she's moving south of Tallahassee. I'm guessing she's in a car."

"Let's go."

Dominic beat him to the driver's side of the US Marshals' vehicle and held the handle fast. "You ride. I'll drive. We don't have time to argue."

Jake considered doing just that, but he could tell by Dominic's no-nonsense look that he wasn't going to budge. He probably had a point. Jake would probably drive like a maniac to get to Mackenzie and put all of their lives in danger.

Jake met Dominic's eye. "She means something to me," he said quietly. It was hard for him to admit, but Dominic needed to know. This was more than just a case. His heart was also invested. He didn't want to hide anything from his team.

Dominic nodded, his expression deadly serious. "I know, Jake. I get it. Trust me."

Jake nodded and moved to the other side of the car, not needing to say anything more. Just as he slammed the passenger-side door, Chris and Whitney joined them in the back seat and Dominic hit the gas and spun the tires. The car turned, fishtailed and headed out the driveway, leaving a plume of dust behind them.

Thirty minutes later, they were still driving south of town. Max was whimpering now and had sunk farther down in the seat. As terrified as she was, Mackenzie's heart went out to the teenager. It must be a really scary thing to be alone in the world in the first place, but to be facing death at such a young age must be even more horrifying. She reached over with her bound hands and touched his leg, but he pulled back even farther and wouldn't allow the contact.

"You're going to be okay," she whispered. "We'll make it out of this somehow."

Taylor must have overheard her because the next thing she knew, she heard his raucous voice booming from the front seat. "You shouldn't lie to the boy like that, *Ms. Weaver.*" He said her name with a biting tone, making it perfectly clear that he now knew her identity and was aware of the mistake he'd made the first time by not killing her when he'd had the opportunity. "You'll be dead in less than an hour. If I were you, I'd start remembering all the good times in my life. There aren't going to be any more."

She cringed at his words and then stiffened her spine. She refused to give up hope. The situation looked bleak, but with God, anything was possible. Wasn't it? She held on to that small bit of hope, squeezing her eyes shut and praying again. She had to admit she had no idea how to get out of this situation. This was one problem she couldn't fix on her own. *God, please help us.*

The car slowed, and Taylor turned off to the right, following a narrow paved road that eventually turned into sand. It led through a forest of planted pines and scrub oaks, and Mackenzie thought they must be in a very private area again, because she didn't see a single house or other vehicle along their trek. Finally, Taylor stopped the car and parked, and the two men got out and pulled Mackenzie and Max out of the car. Max started crying, and Taylor pulled out his gun and struck the boy on the forehead. "Shut up and take it like a man," Taylor grunted. "It was your choice to sell us out. Now live with the consequences of your actions."

"Or die with them," Lager added with a smile.

Taylor joined in on the laugh and then pushed the two toward a path that led off the road to the right and into the trees. Max was silent now, and blood was dripping down his eyebrow onto his cheek. Again, Mackenzie felt compassion for him as her mind whirled on an escape strategy. Was there any way out of this? She thought of Jake. How she wished she had told him her plans to meet with Max! But no, she had made a hasty mistake, and now she was going to pay for that with her life. She felt a hole in her heart and realized she'd overlooked something else. She had never told Jake she loved him. She wasn't sure when the feelings had really taken root, but that kiss on his couch had sealed the deal. And now he would never know. She would never get to share her feelings with him or see his glass-green eyes light up at her proclamation. She had lost her opportunity, and it was all because of her own rash mistake.

They stumbled along the path, and Mackenzie moved as slowly as possible, knowing that whenever they reached their destination, her life would be over. Twice she fell, and twice Taylor jerked her back to her feet. Finally, they came to a clearing, and the trees gave way to a giant hole in the ground filled with water. It had been a while since she had seen a sinkhole, and this one was surrounded by rock and sandy walls, with bits of brush and other plants lining the rim. The water below was black, and Mackenzie cringed, afraid to know what types of Florida wildlife were living in the murky depths. Snakes and alligators leaped to mind, so if a bullet or the fall didn't kill her, the animals were sure to get a free meal.

"Well, princess, I'd love to stay and get to know you better, but we have a tight schedule to keep," Taylor said as he winked at her. He ran his finger down her cheek again in an intimate motion, and she jerked away from his touch and nearly fell into the sinkhole in her attempt to get away from him. Taylor grabbed her arm and pulled her back. "Not yet. Don't worry, that sinkhole is going to be your final resting place, but not before I put some hot lead in you. I need to make sure you don't reappear again."

He stepped back, pulled out his gun and pointed it at her forehead. "Goodbye, Mackenzie Weaver."

The gunshot cracked through the air, but Mackenzie didn't feel the bullet enter her body. The shock of still being alive was instant and nearly overwhelming. She glanced at Taylor and watched as his eyes dimmed, his hand dropped the gun into the sand, and then his body slowly careened into the sinkhole behind her. A few seconds later she heard a large splash from below.

Out of the corner of her eye, she noticed Max escaping into the brush. At the same time, Lager grabbed her roughly and pulled her in front of him, effectively using her as a shield.

She screamed but was instantly silenced by Lager pressing his gun against her back. They were still only a few steps away from the precipice.

"Let her go, Lager, or you're next." Jake's commanding voice was like steel, yet Lager only laughed.

"I doubt you're willing to kill her, and that's what will happen if you aim for me. I'm leaving here right now, and I'm taking her with me. She's my ticket to freedom."

Mackenzie felt an instant sense of relief at hearing Jake's voice, despite Lager's tone and the gun being pointed at her back. Suddenly, she knew she had an opportunity to survive this encounter. "Do it, Jake," she yelled. She wasn't sure where Jake was hiding, but she knew he had to be in hearing distance. "Take the shot. I trust you."

Lager tightened his grip. "Shut up or I'll kill you right now," he growled in her ear.

"Do it, Jake," she said again, ignoring Lager's threat. Her voice was more confident this time. "Shoot now."

Suddenly, Mackenzie saw Jake emerge from the trees, a high-powered rifle pointed directly at Lager. Behind him and slightly to the left stood Dominic, his weapon also pointed at Lager. Both were wearing their vests and looked incredibly deadly. Although she didn't see them, Mackenzie was sure that Chris and Whitney were nearby as well, also armed and ready to shoot.

"I'm getting out of here," Lager yelled. "I'm going…"

The shot was deafening, and Mackenzie actually felt the air displace as the bullet traveled by her ear and hit Derek Lager. His grip on her loosened and then fell away completely as Lager crumpled into a bloody heap on the ground beside her.

Her entire body started shaking, and she wiped away some of the blood that had spattered on her cheek. A few seconds later, Jake approached and swept her into his arms, pulling her well away from the edge of the sinkhole.

"I was so scared," he murmured, kissing her gently on her lips. "I didn't want to lose you."

"I knew you'd save me. The minute I heard your voice, I knew everything was going to be okay."

His embrace grew stronger. "I love you, Mackenzie. I don't want to keep going on in this world without you."

"You won't," she said fiercely, clinging to her man. "Because I love you right back."

EPILOGUE

Three months later

J.T. Austin raised his hands and whistled. "Okay, everyone, settle down." He waited for a moment or two as the group of deputy marshals stopped their conversations, found their seats and gave him their attention. "As you all know, Mackenzie Weaver recently finished her documentary on our US Marshals unit, and it's due to air next Friday on prime time. However—" He had to stop as cheers and clapping erupted. "However," he continued once the noise had died down, "I thought it might be nice for us to preview the film first since it was created right here in our own backyard with Jake Riley and his team." He pointed to Jake, who stood and joined J.T. at the front of the room with Mackenzie at his side. Once again, the room broke out in applause.

Jake smiled and waved at them to settle down. "When Mackenzie Weaver first showed up with her camera, I thought it was the worst possible thing that could happen."

His comment was met with boos and hisses from the crowd, but Mackenzie just laughed as Jake started smiling himself. "However, now I realize that God had intervened in my life and brought me the most amazing woman I've ever known. I also want you, my family, to be the first to know that we got engaged last night."

The gathering cheered, and Dominic and the rest of his team came up and started patting him on the back and offering both of them their congratulations. Jake couldn't remember being happier in his entire life. The last three months had been like a roller coaster of thrills and delight as he had gotten to know Mackenzie Weaver even better. Both of them had rededicated themselves to God at church, and with Dominic and his wife's help, they had found and joined a home fellowship and were slowly making positive changes in their lives. Jake was beginning to see beauty again in the things around him and God's hand in the blessings in his life. He had a new vigor and excitement for his job as well and had found a new happiness that had eluded him before. Mackenzie was also growing and had recently shared with him how she was finally letting go of a need to control everything and was depending more on God to play an active role in her life choices. She'd finally admitted that she couldn't do everything by herself and had spoken at their home fellowship about how God was teaching her that it was okay to let others help her reach her goals. The last three months had already been a tremendous learning experience for both of them, and they were both committed to continuing down this path of including God in their life and building their relationship on a strong foundation through Christ.

Finally, the cheering died down, the group returned to their seats and the film started rolling. Jake thought back to the Lager case that had done so much to bring him and Mackenzie together. Both Derek Lager and Bryson Taylor had died at the sinkhole, and due to Jake and his team's diligence, they had uncovered and stopped a huge forgery and theft operation. Upon further investigation, they had verified that Beckett was using the copy machines to steal personal information. Lager was then using that information to create fake credit cards and driver's licenses. He'd hired the homeless youth and others to use the falsified credentials and make large purchases of jewelry and electronics at a variety of retail stores, storing the stolen goods at various warehouses. Lager hadn't confined his theft to Tallahassee and had also been operating in Georgia, Alabama and southern Florida. Once he obtained a large enough amount of stolen merchandise, he'd sold the lot to the highest bidder. All in all, the operation had resulted in the arrest of fourteen people and the recovery of over six million dollars' worth of goods. It was a huge multistate win for the US Marshals.

Mackenzie was sitting beside Jake, and he squeezed her hand before turning his attention back to the movie. There were catcalls and other remarks as various team members were featured, but once the credits rolled, Mackenzie was treated to a standing ovation.

Jake hadn't participated in the editing of the movie on purpose because he'd wanted to see it for the first time tonight with the rest of his team. He was truly glad he had waited. The film was better than he had ever imagined it could be. He turned to Mackenzie and met her eyes. "That was simply amazing," he said softly. "It wasn't just a documentary. It was art. You didn't just report the facts, you captured the spirit of the team. How'd you do that?"

Mackenzie smiled, basking in the glow of his compliment. He could tell that his words had touched her, but they were the truth. Her film was truly outstanding.

"I had the best inspiration," she smiled. "I had you."

* * * * *

COMING NEXT MONTH FROM
Love Inspired® Suspense

Available July 2, 2019

DEEP UNDERCOVER
True Blue K-9 Unit • by Lenora Worth
In order to take down a serial bomber, NYPD K-9 officers Brianne Hayes and Gavin Sutherland must go undercover—as a married couple. But with the bomber targeting them to halt the investigation, can they and their K-9 partners find the culprit in time to save their own lives?

NANNY WITNESS
The Baby Protectors • by Hope White
When someone breaks in and puts their lives in danger, nanny Carly Winslow grabs the child in her care and flees—straight into the protective arms of the baby's uncle. Now Detective Brody Whittaker will do anything to keep Carly and his niece safe from a determined kidnapper.

COLD CASE SECRETS
True North Heroes • by Maggie K. Black
Solving his sister's murder is Mountie Jacob Henry's only priority—until his daring helicopter rescue of Grace Finch leaves them stranded in the woods during a storm with escaped convicts in pursuit. Soon he's torn between a future with the beautiful reporter and the painful past he can never forget.

AMISH COVERT OPERATION
by Meghan Carver
After Amish widow Katie Schwartz's search for her reclusive brother results in a shooting and a cryptic message, she must rely on ICE agent Adam Troyer to shield her. But can they work together to bring down the smugglers in Amish country?

RISKY RETURN
Covert Operatives • by Virginia Vaughan
When a teen she's been mentoring is abducted, Rebecca Mason stumbles across a human trafficking ring that wants to permanently silence her. And Collin Walsh, the man she married in secret years ago before he left her to join the military, is suddenly her self-appointed protector.

INHERITED THREAT
by Jane M. Choate
Reeling from the news of her estranged mother's murder, army ranger Laurel Landry returns home to uncover why she was killed—but now someone is after Laurel. To survive, she needs help, so she hires bodyguard Mace Ransom to join her in exposing the crime family that wants her dead.

SPECIAL EXCERPT FROM

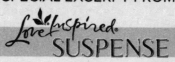
Love Inspired
SUSPENSE

*With a bomber targeting New York City, two K-9 cops
will have to go undercover as a married couple to put
an end to an explosive crime spree.*

Read on for a sneak preview of
Deep Undercover *by Lenora Worth,
the next exciting installment to the*
True Blue K-9 Unit *miniseries, available
July 2019 from Love Inspired Suspense.*

K-9 officer Gavin Sutherland held tight to his K-9 partner
Tommy's leash and scanned the crowd, his mind on high
alert, his whole body tense as he tried to protect the city
he loved. People from all over the world stood shoulder
to shoulder along the East River, waiting for the annual
Fourth of July fireworks display.

His partner, a black-and-white springer spaniel, knew
the drill. Tommy worked bomb detection. He had been
trained to find incendiary devices. He knew to sniff the air
and the ground. Sniff, sit, repeat. Be rewarded.

Glancing up, Gavin spotted his backup, K-9 officer
Brianne Hayes, a rookie who had been paired with him to
continue gaining experience.

Brianne headed toward him, her auburn hair caught up
in a severe bun. That fire-colored hair matched her fierce
determination to prove herself since she was one of only a
few female K-9 officers in the city that never slept.

Brianne's partner, Stella, was also in training with the K-9 handlers.

"I've been along the perimeters of the park," Brianne said. "Nothing out of the ordinary. Can't wait for the show."

Scanning the area again, he said, "I think the crowd grows every year. Standing room only tonight."

"Stella keeps fidgeting and sniffing. She needs to get used to this."

Stella stopped and lifted her nose into the air, a soft growl emitting from her throat.

"Steady, girl. You'll need to contain that when the fireworks start."

But Stella didn't quit. The big dog tugged forward, her nose sniffing both air and ground.

Gavin watched the Labrador, wondering what kind of scent she'd picked up. Then Tommy alerted, going still except for his wagging tail that acted like a warning flag, his body trembling in place.

"Something's up," Gavin whispered to Brianne. "He's picked up a signature somewhere."

Brianne whispered low. "There's a bomb?"

Don't miss
Deep Undercover *by Lenora Worth,*
available July 2019 wherever
Love Inspired® Suspense books and ebooks are sold.

www.LoveInspired.com